Frisco I:
Misfits

Sean A. Labbé

ISBN-13:978-1729763858
ISBN-10:1729763855

For Fidan, Brendan, and Hope

STORIES

A special thanks to Elissa Goldman for editing these stories. Thanks also to my wife Fidan and my son Brendan for their help, especially with some of the titles.

HAPPY NEW YEAR

The party is over, Jason thought, but nobody knows. Deep in his head, a cog turned, a tumbler clicked. It took great effort for him to peel apart his lids. He glimpsed himself in the glass of the balcony door. He slumped crossways on the hide-a-bed, legs dangling over the back, like a high-jumper who'd attempted a Fosbury Flop. Everything was upside-down. The crown of Jason's head smushed against the floor, his feet seemed nearly to touch the ceiling, which was ten feet away. From his viewpoint, the record player was upside down as well. A song managed to play, even upside down, the bass tentatively layering the floor with sound, um-humming. Like a toy musical train, the guitar chords took their time, coaxing him to come along and for a moment he thought a dozen turntables spun the same record simultaneously.

"We are monads," lulled the record, "in our windowless house. We are monads..."

The voice spoke more than sang, talking then growing quiet. The refrain swayed to the slowed-down tempo and droned "monads." The word jumped around in his head, like a yo-yo. Jason's eyes strained after the sound. Something told him to get up. He sucked in his belly. His thighs refused to budge; needles pricked his toes. He tucked in his knees then tipped his body up into a quasi-headstand. Jason felt like a diver jumping off a high board, frantically straightening his posture before he knifed into the water. The walls drifted. He was slipping; dislocated, he plunged through himself and grabbed at the floor smashing up at him.

I never blacked out, Jason thought, or did I? He was lying face-down on wood planks that smelled like smoldering dirt. When he lifted his chin blood dribbled on the floor. Jason rolled over. He inched up on his elbows and took stock of his body. Cigarette ash speckled his navy twills and his flannel shirt was damp. The elastic of his boxers was exposed. He tasted blood-flavored spit, and he swallowed, tasting rusty iron. His lip had puffed up. He tongued the gouge then cringed: it smarted like a razor nick stung by sweat.

A willowy girl in a charcoal turtleneck glided past Jason as he lay on the floor. She walked over to the record player and tapped her foot. If the song was what yearning sounded like, she was how yearning looked. Jason squinted at her scrap of a face, her pink cheeks. She dinged a bell in him and he knew he looked befuddled: his brain riffled a rolodex for her name but came up blank. Surely they had talked that night. He remembered telling her not to worry: he was drinking inadequately to get really drunk, pacing his intake meticulously. But he had let her slip back into her clique, and he had moped, downing more tumblers of red wine than he ever intended and puffing away on cigarettes that kept appearing between his fingers. The girl turned the record off, her turtleneck rode up her pasty back. She placed the record, minus the sleeve, back inside its cover: murky night sea, a spotlight, the group's name spelled in block letters: (We Are) The Missing Chums.

Then somebody put on REM's *Green* album again. They'd played songs from it a lot that evening, cueing "Orange Crush," "Get up," "I Remember California" three or four times apiece. The last song played now in the background, and Jason's head quavered with the memory of the vocals. The singer berated him as a nearly-was, an almost-ran. Then the needle hissed and popped in the run-out groove. The party-goers started to chant loudly. When Jason realized they were counting down the seconds to midnight, he balled his hands and lowered his head. When the revelers shouted two, Jason's body shifted, and at the count of one, he was sitting against the hide-a-bed.

They stopped counting after one; nobody shouted zero. Time became a dead spot. After a while, they bellowed "happy new year!" Jason watched them hooray and twirl ratcheting noisemakers. Paper tubes uncurled limply, somebody played a loudmouth kazoo. Nobody noticed Jason and people started stepping on him. A heel landed an inch from his hand; a toe punted his thigh. Somebody knelt beside him and he saw the willowy girl again. She blushed and her face stayed red, as if she were continuously embarrassed. Mascara clumps on her eyelids, she crouched down low beside him and pried open his lids. She cradled his head and spread his hair with her fingers.

"How do you feel?" Her voice squeaked like balloons rubbing together.

"Okay," Jason said.

He didn't remember the rest of their conversation from before, so he started over. Did he tell her about the flight? He spent a whole afternoon going five-hundred miles per hour, watching the wings slash piles of cloud. He watched the farms crawl by below him. The endless prairie struck him dumb with awe but soon its vastness smothered him and he wanted the plane to land. Why did he come? He told her. Back home, he was regarded as a weirdo. There was no place for him. He never belonged. When he thought he'd found somebody weird like him, she'd only gape at him with a look that said, I might be weird but I'm not as weird as this guy. He was told that here they were open-minded. So he decided to visit his buddy Mitch, from back home, who had moved to the Bay Area a while ago. For the time being, Jason explained, he was staying with Mitch and his girlfriend in their one-bedroom. Still suffering from jet-lag, Jason said, still adjusting to the shift in time zones. Each night he crashed at ten on this convertible foam chair, which transformed into a narrow cot, while Mitch and the girlfriend watched movies on the VCR. But Jason's eyes snapped wide at 5:00 a.m. every morning. Nobody is ever awake, Jason said. He remembered how he would try to go back to sleep, flopping and thrashing; how, eventually, he would doze off for a short while, and when his eyes drifted open again, the window shades glowed white: little use against the intense morning sun. And Jason would lie there, head sore and neck stiff, kidneys aching, wondering if he'd made a mistake in coming.

As Jason wrapped up his tale, the girl fiddled with the collar of her turtleneck, unrolling it partway under her chin. "You know where Mitch went?"

Jason craned his neck. "I think he left with his girlfriend, what's-her-name."

She tilted her head. "That's her? No way. Really?"

"Maybe they're not soul mates. But they live together and sleep in the same bed."

"He seemed pretty available."

"He's friendly, but he's also a very loyal friend."

"Well, that's unfortunate," she said. She batted her lashes. They fluttered like moths trapped in a window.

Jason drew in his lip. "I'm not seeing anybody," he said. He became silent then.

The muscles of the girl's face tensed visibly, like a hand tightening. After a minute, she dipped her head and half-smiled. "You seem so needy," she said then hiccupped. She stifled her laughter. Jason curled the corners of his mouth, baring his teeth. He did his best to laugh. But then he winced and licked the cut in his mouth, trying to keep the spot wet with his tongue.

Then somebody switched off the lights. A smoky fog flooded the room: instantaneous black. In the dark the people's head became plum blobs. A let-down "aw" caromed off the walls. As Jason tongued the sore lip, the girl shifted at his side. Shoes scuffed the floor. She was gone. After a minute, the bulb flickered on, and Jason squinted in the glare. Hair tousled, Mitch cuddled the willowy girl in her turtleneck at the threshold. Thigh poked between her knees, hands cupping haunches, he shoved her body against the wall: the "monster mash." He mouthed her throat and face. His sweat-stringy hair laced her cheeks. Black clumps seeped from her lids, trailing down her face like tears made of coal.

The room went dark again. When the lights came back on, the willowy girl was leading Mitch away. At the door stood a woman outfitted in black leggings and a plaid skirt, clutching the album cover.

"I need you guys to go," she said, "before somebody calls the cops."

Jason watched as nobody moved. The woman swung the door and wedged a rubber stop under the edge. A couple partiers slinked toward the pile of coats. A scrawny fellow with long chestnut hair donned a glittery top hat and, after pecking the woman's cheek, touched his chest and vanished. The woman hunched her shoulders. Jason saw partiers bumble in groups; he saw them filter out single-file. The coat-tree tottered as they jerked garments off, stripping the prongs clean. Heads shaking, the people who stayed frowned. Jason frowned too. One guy yanked his sleeve up and tapped his wrist. Maybe they should go to Trader Sam's. Heads were shaking. Nobody goes there. Eyes scanned the ceiling. Blarney Stone? Nag's Head? Remember last year? Crowds mobbed the entrances. In places the lines extended down a block. When the doors swung open, voices roared and hollered. People drank in the toilets: absolute bedlam. Jason only listened; he wished he knew these places.

"What about Decatur Street?"

"Went out of business."

"Never closed. Now under new management."

"They call it, The Creeping Damp."

"Creeping Dump's more like it."

"They serve goblets. I'm not exaggerating. They're as big as your head."

Now the people moved. They exited. Jason felt as though he were still on the airplane and he saw himself crouched under the overhead, waiting for a break in the passengers hurtling down the aisle. He was knocked by the party-goers' knees and elbows. When a space cleared on the floor, he tied to stand. His momentum ebbed and his rump sagged down. Somebody cackled. He made a spectacle all right; nineteen, a physical wreck. He looked like somebody doing a push-up backwards. At first, he scuttled on palms and heels. With each faltering movement of his arm, his shoulders clunked. Then somehow he managed to snap himself upright. He had a headache: pinging, knocking. After waiting out the pain, he took a step. Though his legs quaked, he kept his footing. The carpet, strewn with heaps of litter, seemed to squirm. When he shrugged his weight forward, his toe clipped an ashtray, and bent cigarette butts, smeared with lipstick, skidded across the carpet. He sidestepped a jug of green glass with an inch of wine in the bottom. But then something squished under his feet; he had trampled a pizza box, splotched and gooey with congealed cheese drippings.

By the time Jason reached the bathroom, he'd lost his balance and he landed on the floor. The sink stood apart from the wall. No mirror hung above it, no medicine cabinet, only a chalky rectangle of primer and corner screws: a picture of nothing. Even without checking, he knew how he looked. He imagined his eyes had bags under them, and were bloodshot and watery to boot. He flashed a smile of short stubby teeth. He clumsily turned the antique cross handles on the sink. For a minute, Jason washed his face, running the water over his palms till his skin squeaked. Cupping water, he gulped, then filled his mouth and swished it around in his cheeks. He attempted to tamp down unruly tufts of hair. He doubted it did any good: he still pictured disobedient clumps atop his head. A stray twinge went through him. The ache knocked tentatively to see if anybody was home. He gripped his temples to hold the pieces of his skull together.

When Jason returned to the kitchen, a bunch of partiers tapped the table with spoons. Mitch chugged from a large bottle of vodka, tilting his whole body backwards. Then he wiped his mouth and kicked a tumbler across the floor.

"Olé!" he shouted: "olé–olé–olé, olé, olé!"

Mitch jogged in place. Everyone laughed. My buddy, Jason thought. He chuckled too. The willowy girl lost her voice chanting along with the group. She cuddled Mitch's arm, slow-dancing against him. Jason tried not to look but he saw them shimmy along the table, bobbing their heads. When Jason glanced away, the woman dressed in the black leggings and the plaid skirt came to his side and yelled in his ear.

"That song is so old and dumb and lame," she said. "I hate it. I don't know why they keep singing it."

When Jason shook his head, his skull rattled with pain. He barely listened to the woman talking. The song dated back to last summer, she said, when they haunted an Irish pub. You know the sort: crotchety old men with lumpy faces sit stoop-shouldered at the bar, mahogany booths, walls hung with posters of mystical Eire, eight-by-tens of Joyce, Beckett, Yeats, the tricolor. Sidewalk outside lacquered with barf, piss, blood. The owner, a stout matron with a cropped hairdo, installed a jumbo screen and for a month straight kept the channel tuned to soccer matches while her pug slept by the fireplace. That was when they latched on to the cheer and made it their thing.

"Never understood," the woman said. "Nobody's Irish. I mean, everybody is, well, as much as anybody is." She frowned. "I mean: no more than anybody else." She was chopping the air with her hands then shouting: "I doubt they even care much for soccer either."

The soccer chant was booming now in the stairwell. Then the walls muffled the group's echo. The cheer gradually sounded far away. After a minute, a door swooshed open. The cheer hovered, as if the group rode a hot-air balloon in the canyon made by the buildings. The cheer soared. It fluttered. It seemed to hang in the middle of the air before swooping down. When it tapered off, Jason stepped to the window. His cheek smearing the pane, he peered into the dark and saw figures lurk noiselessly on the street corner. Two shadows locked their arms and skipped.

A tickle in Jason's throat made him cough and he clenched his fists. A wandering pebble pinged hard inside his head and he squeezed his eyes shut for a moment. When he opened them again, the room stood nearly empty. A girl with a wheat ponytail stooped, draping a scarf round a squat guy's humped shoulders. The woman in the black leggings dumped a pair of duck-boots at the guy's feet. Jason stared at this mysterious silent trio. When the knocking inside Jason's head eased up, he asked them, did they know what happened to Mitch? Nobody could tell him. Mitch was there five minutes ago then maybe he skipped out? The squat guy saw him leave with the girl in the turtleneck: Lorna. The trio mentioned some bars and Jason remembered their names but he didn't know where they were or how to reach them. Jason gazed forlornly at them and they asked him where he stayed. With Mitch, he said. They asked Jason if he could find his way. He scrunched his face then shook his head no. They didn't know Mitch's address. Jason told them about the wide street and the block-long brick building and the white-frame hospital with the tinted windows.

"I know where you mean," the girl said. "It's pretty much a straight shot. We can get you there halfway. You're welcome if you want to tag along."

The squat guy turned to the woman. "We're gone. Out of here. Bye."

The woman waved at them from the top landing. When they stepped outside and Jason looked up, the lights in the apartment went out.

The pair, the squat guy and the ponytailed girl, easily outpaced Jason even though they dawdled, their stride slow and indecisive. The guy's duck boots squeaked endlessly. Even in the dark, Jason saw the girl's ponytail. That thick bundle of hair swung and swished rapidly despite her steady gait. Flat-footed, Jason straggled, not limping, but his legs stutter-stepped. Every couple minutes he looked up and saw them standing, half-turned, gesturing at him. His head burned with confusion. He groped along the flat fronts of the two-story buildings that walled the block. The pair wandered up a hill and stopped at a park. Jason hurried before they strolled away and left him alone in the night. Finally he caught them as they reached a broad boulevard that dipped down for a mile. Y-shaped masts lined the median. Each crossbar held globe-shaped lamps, tinting the fog orange. The sky smoldered but a chill breeze goaded him onward. Despite a shiver, Jason lengthened his step and as he moved his legs limbered and soon he drew abreast of the pair. The girl, holding her ponytail, was telling about the neighborhood. She pointed across the street at a diner with a yellow plate glass window. Two patrolmen sipped coffee at the counter in their dark blues and a television flickered in the corner, oddly calm for this night of all nights.

"They're open twenty-four hours," she said. "Pulled many all-nighters, studying: notes strewn everywhere, teeth clamping a yellow highlighter: nobody asked me to leave."

She trailed off. Jason pictured her in a booth with the notes and the highlighter. He listened for more but she stopped talking and he did not say anything back. What could he say? He cut glances to his side at the row of businesses they were passing. They had narrow storefronts, each with a padlocked metal gate shut tight across the entry, built wall-to-wall with no alley to separate them. They stopped at the corner of the street and waited for the light to change in their favor. In the space of a minute, several shapes staggered from the trees near the corner and then jaywalked across the street. The shapes hooted. They chased after a bus, slapping the door. Somehow they flagged down a taxi, which did a U-turn.

With a wave, the guy in the duck-boots peeled away from them, and Jason could hear the soles of his boots squeaking on the pavement then stop. A gate clanged shut.

Jason looked at the girl's ponytail but said nothing. Two blocks later she stopped walking.

"This is my street," she said, "I live halfway down." She stood on her tiptoes to give Jason a friendly hug just as he leaned over to reciprocate her gesture, and her chin bonked his forehead.

"Oh, I'm sorry." She swatted his shoulder with the flat of her hand.

Her warmth heated his cheek. A taxi screeched by, windows halfway down: the occupants chanted the soccer cheer.

"I'd invite you in for a coffee," she said, "but I have to work in four hours."

"Some happy new year," Jason said, "huh?"

She shook her head. "It's good luck: you work on the first, you'll work the whole year. So they say."

Jason gazed helplessly as she went home. Along the street, a beer can clattered emptily.

"You know where you are?" she asked, turning and walking backwards.

Jason glanced ahead. Several blocks down, an

accordion bus rumbled away from the curb, cutting off the taxi. The car's horn honked.

"Think so," he said. "See you around."

Jason stood there feeling dumb because she probably would have given him her number if he'd had enough sense to ask. He set off. He found his stride and walked each block in a minute and soon he reached his corner. Jason stopped in front of a medical apparel store. A mannequin in a white button-front dress stood in the window with her arms crossed, a twin-winged hat perched atop her smooth-featured head. Across the street, a crowd of partiers, suburbanites, he guessed, in town for a spree, filled the sidewalk. A person in the group whooped a dingbat shriek. Then the soccer cheer broke out again. The cheer flitted from one person to another and Jason focused his hearing. He thought he heard Mitch. The pebble that pinged inside his head became a slow, dull pain, creeping down into his jawbones. The mannequin stared blankly at him. It's late, Jason thought. I'm worn out. It's cold.

When he reached the front steps of Mitch's building, he lingered for a moment, happy he made it back. Home, sort of. It was like pulling in the garage and switching off your car: no rush to get out, no rush to go in. The old wooden building, set ten feet back from the curb. No alley or path separated the structures. The flanking buildings edged forward. The frame drooped. The windows seemed cockeyed. Feet had worn bare the stones paving the alcove. A jealously private place, that's what he thought, standing in the entryway. He could barely see. Overhead, a yellow forty-watt smoldered, a fly-specked bulb shedding fuzzy light. Painted black, the push-button doorbells studded a shoebox-sized plate on the wall. A strip of plastic tape hung crookedly beneath each button: there were the embossed digits, the alphabetical characters: unpronounceable Russian or Vietnamese last names.

Jason shoved his hand into his pocket and clenched the keys in his fist. The new metal glinted as he fingered the cuts. He traced the leading edge, as ridged and jagged as a map of the coast of California.

He settled the tip into the keyway. The blade missed the slot and he tried again. When the blade slid inside, he wiggled it in his hand. He torqued his wrist. Something clicked, like snapping a crayon or a bar of chocolate, and the key jumped. The metal broke and he backed away holding the bow of the key with no blade. He tapped his foot and, huffing, knelt, looking through the keyhole. Jason could see a glint of the broken key lodged in there. He plucked at it with his fingernails. What are you trying to grab? You'd need a pair of tweezers to get the piece out. They'd have to call a locksmith. Jason heaved a shove at the door; solid as a fortress gate, it pushed him back. He dropped the broken key and walked down the steps, away from the building. He leaned on a parked car and something chirped. He leaped back and went to the middle of the street. Standing there he could see the light was on in Mitch's apartment. Jason cupped his hands, fashioned after a megaphone, and attempted to yell up to Mitch. His voice squeaked and cut out. Then Jason found loose gravel and clasping a chunk tossed it at Mitch's window. He missed and it clacked against the wood. He found a bottle cap and threw it up at the window but it didn't hit hard enough to be noticed, tinkling shyly on the glass.

Jason tried ringing up to Mitch's apartment again. He thought he had the right button and pressed it hard. He felt the doorbell buzz, ringing somewhere. He felt pretty sure he knew it worked. He thought back to the day he showed up. The doorbell worked then. It works. Jason tried Mitch's button again. He inhaled deeply while he waited for a response. Nobody answered. When he exhaled, breath emerged in shreds. Maybe the connection was faulty? Had he heard the doorbell ring? He shook his head. Audibly, he counted to ten and waited before he pressed the button again. Nothing, nobody answered. He rang every doorbell. Still. Not a sound. Nothing. No. Answer.

The pebble in his brain started rolling around again. He slouched along the brick building, trailed by feelings of loneliness. At the corner, he halted. For several minutes he stared at the shop window letting the skinny nurse-mannequin scold him non-verbally. Two payphones stood mounted back-to-back on the sidewalk. He lifted the first phone's receiver and heard nothing. He cradled the phone and rubbed his hands. The other phone's receiver hung off the hook but once he pushed the cradle down the dial tone hummed. He plunked a nickel and a dime into the slot. He punched Mitch's number. The voice told him to deposit five more cents to complete his call. He fished, plunked in another nickel. He connected to Mitch's phone and a muted pulsing sounded in his ear. In his mind's eye, he envisioned the room: where did Mitch keep the phone? He tried to remember. Did they have an answering machine? He hung up and tried again. The answering machine picked up and a voice read the phone number then beeped, prompting Jason to leave a message.

"Hello," he blurted, "locked out—"

The connection died. The dial tone howled in the earpiece. He smashed the handset into the cradle. Like a low-voltage shock, a shiver oozed through him. His body shuddered. His teeth knocked. He palmed his heated forehead. Was a hotel out of the question? He barely remembered how much cash he had on him but he doubted it would cover the cost of a room. He removed his wallet and as he counted the bills a scrap of paper fluttered down: a receipt from Jack in the Box. Still the white-dressed mannequin looked impassively at him from her window. If he retraced his steps, he could find the street of the girl with the ponytail. Swaying, he shook his head: the houses all looked alike.

Then he heard the soccer chant break out again. The sound formed membranes in the air, and the words looked like a bunch of party balloons. The chant gained momentum and rode high into the air, then dropped back down to Jason's level. He chased the chanting, never thinking he would catch it, but his reflexes had taken over.

The chant stopped at the doorway of an Irish pub. A crush of bodies gathered at the door of the bar, the revelers swayed, singing the cheer, then disappeared into the pub. When Jason reached the swing doors, the cheering stopped. He heard snatches of it and the sound strung him along. He looked around the interior for the wannabe soccer hooligans. A square seating area adjoined a narrow room with a counter and stools.

On the wall hung faded posters of stone bridges and whitewashed cottages with thatched roofs. Four men shot pool at a table. In the corner, a pug sprawled by the fireplace, stick legs, balloon-belly, and a man crouched, knock-kneed, at a jukebox. Aged men sat stoop-shouldered at the counter. They weren't chanting and spoke under their breath, snipping their words. The chant began again and when Jason looked in the direction of the chanter he thought he saw a smattering of faces from the party, but the regular crowd stared at them. He'd visited this kind of murky dive bar before, with the regulars-only. It was the local watering hole, populated by townies, louts, and troublemakers. They looked like the kind of people whose eye you avoided catching, if you had an ounce of sense.

Jason took a seat at the bar and chomped on a salt cracker. The bartender eyed Jason's fake license. He watched bodies yank past him from the counter then turned away. The bartender pulled the lever of the tap handle. Frothy beer gushed into a globe-shaped glass and the barman eased the tap handle up and lopped the foam with a flat stick. The suds went down the overflow grate. He handed the pint to Jason. A shamrock was cut into the thick foam. Jason placed four singles on the edge of the counter then folded the bills lengthwise and stuck the money between his fingers. The bartender's head nodded slightly. Chocolate vinegar flooded Jason's mouth, like cold black coffee. The drink whooshed down, no tiny bubbles pricked his throat. Some more people entered the bar and Jason thought he remembered them from the party, but Mitch was not with them. Jason saw no recognition of himself in their looks and glances. The newbies began chatting with the bartender.

"You want to watch the tape?"

They nodded and the barman reached under the counter and pointed a remote control in the air. For a moment, the jumbo screen glowed blue and then soccer players tapped a ball with their insteps before sprinting across a green pitch. Everybody all together hoisted their pints and cheered even though nothing had happened. The party jigged about the bar stools, hoarsely braying the chant at the top of their lungs. A gray old man swiveled back on his stool, crooked his elbows and hunkered protectively over his beer.

They played the match in a continuous loop on the screen. The regulars took timid sips. Jason ordered a second pint. His headache was ebbing. For minutes on end, he forgot about the pain till a ripple prodded his brain. When the partiers chanted the cheer, the locals declined to join in. The regular boozers cracked jokes about bars with fern plants and snooty yuppies straying from where they belonged. When a stubbly-faced oldster glared at Jason, he shrugged then drank slowly from his pint. When he glanced back, the man's eyes had narrowed to slits. Nobody took the hint. The group kept chanting. On the screen, Ireland poked the ball in the net. The whole crew erupted. They hopped off the stools, linked arms and jigged, chanting the cheer like patients in a mental institution. The older customers scrutinized them, befuddled. Somebody played a Joe Cocker song on the jukebox. A guitar riff careened through the room and gravelly voice rasped in the hubbub. An old man sat bolt upright. Hands slapped the counter. Then the angry shouting started.

"No Joe Cocker!"

"Who keeps playing that?"

"Turn it off!"

A grizzled old man slid off his stool and marched through the crowd, heading towards the jukebox. He lowered his shoulder and smashed into the machine and hugged it in an attempt to tackle it. He rocked the whole thing back and forth, and the machine tilted up and the song stopped. The man stood back then wiped his forehead with his sleeve, victorious. Somebody in the crowd began to cheer and the stunt earned him a shove. It was too hard. He toppled over backwards. A table fell down. A glass shattered on the floor.

A regular sloshed beer in a guy's face. The bar went silent except for the TV.

Somebody asked: "what gives?"

Nobody said anything, everyone staring at the floor while people squabbled. Sometime later, they piped down. A hand laid a five-dollar bill on the counter that the bartender pushed away. The bartender told Jason to make way: the waitress needed the space. Jason ceded his ground. Over the top of the crowd, he saw the door swing, and the kids funneled out. Jason decided to join the exodus. He made his way steadily towards the exit, but strangers put their arms around his shoulders. The arms tightened like a lariat but then suddenly he was being dragged outside. It was the bouncer, he had pulled Jason and some girl out of the pub.

"The party is over," he said. "You all have to go."

Jason practiced his answer, he wanted to say to them all, no it is not over, I'm only getting started, it's a new beginning. The bouncer swept him with his eyes and jabbed him in the ribs with blunt fingers strong enough to snap an ear of corn. The bouncer's mustache wriggled when his mouth moved. He seemed to be changing his mind about something. He looked up at a short-haired woman watching them from the mezzanine. She nodded.

"Okay," the bouncer said, "but you can't stand here. Are you staying or going?"

The question threw Jason. He tilted his head. He cradled his chin. He played a game of charades by himself. He mimed pondering a question, thinking intently, throwing his arms up and shrugging his shoulders making believe he had no answer yet. Jason needed more time to give the matter of staying or going a lengthier consideration. But he knew. It was more than a premonition or hunch. The knowing crept up on him. Muscle memory, a habit, like knowing the gist of a movie but forgetting the plot. Not going anywhere, he decided. Jason found his voice and began to chant.

"Olé," he sang out. Then at the top of his lungs: "olé–olé–olé!"

Everybody looked at him, very confused. They rushed against him: a mass of limbs and torsos. Outside, he sprawled headlong onto the pavement. Laughter blew up. He scraped his palms while getting up from the sidewalk. The group swarmed him then moved on, morphing into a different shape. A second group stomped the sidewalk, chanting aggressively. Behind him, yet another group yelled the cheer. Jason peered through the bar's window: the regulars remained on their stools. Then Jason decided to follow one of the gangs of soccer fans. At his approach, the chant ceased, and the group disbanded. Somewhere else someone restarted the cheer, so Jason headed for the sound. A half-block away, a group bopped along the sidewalk then ducked round the corner, pulling the chant after them.

"Olé, olé–olé–olé...!"

The sound flew above the buildings.

"...olé..."

Jason reached the corner. The group vanished; their echo retreated, an auditory mirage.

"...olé!"

He glanced around. The sidewalk was empty. The street was deserted. New year, new territory: he was alone.

ROOMIES

Scotty's decision to move to San Francisco wasn't a random impulse. Inklings of a future as an urbanite would stir in him when he rode the bus through the city. Scotty stayed at the beach for hours. He watched sheets of water skate across the sand, and power-kites swarming on the paper-gray horizon. A beach-walker waved. A jogger nodded. Everybody acknowledged him, even a man in a black wetsuit who paddled a surfboard up and over a crashing wave. Scotty found this attention odd because generally he liked nobody and nobody liked him. Scotty walked the beach prying smooth shards of ocean-polished glass, a brick-colored pebble, or a shell from the compacted sand. He kept these objects in a jar in his bedroom, under a window that served as a poster of suburbia. When the water drew closer to the place where Scotty stood, he high-stepped away, then stopped. Once Scotty heard a dog yapping his name. The black lump sprinted over the sand straight at him. It was an impish whiskered squirt of a thing. The tiny terrier frolicked at his feet. Then the dog abruptly twirled and raced back to its owner, who leashed the dog under the retaining wall.

When Scotty watched the dog lose its freedom, in that moment he decided he needed to live somewhere else. Staying in suburbia was the safe choice, the frumpy nice girl who gladly hung out with you, not the total cutie who trapped the breath in your lungs and made your mouth clumsy. Scotty was twenty-one. He'd worked since the age of twelve, and none of his checks had bounced, not a single one. After graduating from high school he attended evening classes at West Valley in Saratoga. The tentative plan was that he would transfer to the state college, but he needed to figure out what major he could stand. When he told people about his plans his voice became apologetic: not even he believed what he said. But now he would take action, he would move to the city, not just talk about it.

A basic room suited him: something like Steve McQueen's apartment in *Bullitt* or Henry Caul's place in *The Conversation* before he gutted the rooms. No bay view was required. He wasn't asking for the world. He scoured the classifieds, ballpoint lassoing ads in blue ink. On the day of a viewing, he'd gel his hair and dress in the daffodil-colored shirt he washed and ironed once a week, olive trousers and caramel ankle-boots with rawhide laces. His initial forays into the apartment rental market left him with unpleasant memories. Mobs of people in a hallway, their hands clutching xeroxed papers. Application forms: grainy, speckled; the original apparently lost, the manager xeroxed a copy, misplaced it, then kept making copies from a different copy every time. The salty ocean-breeze mingled with carpet freshener, and the lingering aroma of roach-fogger. Starkly-lit jerky elevators; flights of creaking stairs; a lobby with metal rods, like fencing sabers, dangling from a strip of bare wood screwed into the wall; paint that made the air taste of chalky antacid tablets; a white-haired man with a pink face huffing, hand flitting along the handrail, loafers crackling on the dirty steps; the inescapable feeling that a person died next door.

Eventually, Scotty's hopes lured him to a rental agency. The broker he talked to was hunched over a black screen. Paper ratcheted out from a clunking dot-matrix printer. The broker ripped the sheet neatly along the perforation. Fill out the rental agreement, the fellow says, but Scotty had no references. No credit card. No job yet. He was persona non grata. Landlords took one look at his application, and his application went to the bottom of the pile. Scotty began scouting neighborhoods, noting xeroxed sheets stapled to telephone poles and For Rent placards set in windows. He called landlords from payphones. After dropping his nickels and dimes into the slot, he dialed the numbers he found on his walks. Few landlords answered the phone, so he left messages on their answering machines, while shots rang out in the background. He went to buildings with For Rent signs in person and huddled in the door of a tenement. Nobody showed up. He doubted he would have ever come either.

Wearing a navy peacoat for armor, Scotty crossed the quad at SF State college, up in the city (he'd transferred despite having nowhere to live yet). The student center looked like a heap of leftover skyscraper parts, stacked on top of each other and bolted to the concrete foundation of the campus. The building was like a bad joke his high school math teacher would make. The ground floor of the student center wiggled into a bloated S-shape. Only the top floor formed a neat quadrilateral but an unlikely pyramid listed steeply from the terrace. Everybody saw something different when they looked at the student center. Some saw the upended stern of a half-foundered ship, but Scotty envisaged an airplane's wing banked in a steep turn crashing into the building.

The college walls shook with the students' grunts and coughs. A pungent odor like ammonia dripped through the air, the rancid smell of the unwashed masses. This was one of the many things that made Scotty loathe people. Scotty went to the community board, searching Roommate Wanted flyers. Scotty mouthed words he read on the signs, his chin tucked down, scribbling frantically on a small pad. He reached up and plucked a sheet from the board as though it was a package of goodies clipped to a rack.

As Scotty recorded contact information in his notebook a face he recognized from somewhere bobbled in the meandering crowd of loners and strays. The guy dressed entirely in gray. He looked like a skinny pigeon. His shirt had mother-of-pearl buttons, he wore acid-washed jeans, frayed at the knees, and faded canvas Hi-Tops the color of oatmeal.

"Hey, I know you." Scotty said to the gray man, but couldn't remember the guy's name. They'd taken a humanities course down at West Valley. The guy sat in the front row and raised his hand all the time. The professor listened to him, head tilted, peering at him. His words clunked like wooden blocks hesitantly stacked by a small child. When he debated a classmate (Beethoven was black? Not. So not.), the professor would sigh and grin brazenly at him and all the kids gaped, awed by his bravado. The expression on their faces said, this is education, happening in our class. The funny thing was that the hand-raising ceased after about the third or fourth week, and the guy coasted for the rest of the semester. The professor never called on him. The look on her face said, I know *he* knows: let me pick on somebody else.

The guy looped the headphones around his neck. "I was talking about you," he said. "Then I look. I'm like, Scotty? Hey, I say. Scotty's here. Didn't I say, damn, but it's Scotty?"

"Me too," Scotty said, "I was like I know this guy." He remembered the name now. "Hello, Noah."

Noah moved the wheel on his Walkman to turn the volume down.

"We wondered what happened to you. I told Bruce, too bad you never met Scotty. You guys are two of a kind, like peas in a pod."

"Correct," Bruce said, appearing from the side of the community board. Suddenly Scotty had the sense he was in the midst of a duel. "Noah's like, good old Scotty. Scotty's going places. The world will learn of Scotty one day. He knows what he wants and he knows how to get it and if you listen to him long enough you want it too."

Scotty managed a half-smile. It sounded like something Scotty would say about Noah: an alright guy who became a shrewd operator if his interests were at stake in any way.

"Are you just transferring now?"

Scotty nodded, without telling Noah any specifics about his plans. He wasn't being secretive, he just didn't have a concrete, coherent plan.

"Stuff tripped me up," Scotty said. "I kept thinking I would never leave, but when I decided I needed to go, things came together, and now I'm here."

The song stopped. Noah fingered the rewind button. "Same old Scotty," he said. "Steadfast: no drama, no melodramatics. He's like no-maintenance."

"And you, the same old Noah, right?" Scotty said.

"You know me, man. I am only myself, nobody else. Don't know how."

Bruce was nodding. "So you moved, right, where did you end up?"

"Nowhere yet," Scotty said, "Still looking, for a studio or one-bedroom."

Noah began climbing the steps of the student center. He asked Scotty about his budget and whistled when Scotty said three-fifty. Scotty felt panicked confusion leak through him. Noah read his face and told him that people paid that much to park a car for the month: outside, in an uncovered lot.

"I was looking downtown," Scotty said. "South of Market, the Mission. I found places." He lowered his head. "Well, nothing special. Actually, they were all pretty abysmal." Scotty told them about the tenement and the shots and the no-show landlord.

"The next thing I know," Scotty said, "a black-and-white cruiser careens past, blaring its siren, trailed by this honking fire engine. Fire, I think. No. Medical emergency. No. Somebody got shot."

Noah guffawed. "Not shot, shot up."

"Correct," Bruce said sardonically. "Paramedics save the junkies for the next overdose."

Noah rolled his eyes. "This scrawny bastard thinks he's going to be a fireman when he grows up."

"I have a plan," Bruce said, "following a strict weight-gain regimen. The problem is I have a high metabolism." He struck a boxer's pose and jabbed. "But I'm like a chimp, strong for my size, much more than I look. Here, hold up your hand."

Bruce's hand moved a few inches but his wrist flicked and the knuckles snapped like a wet towel, stinging Scotty's palm. "Sorry, did it hurt?"

Scotty shrugged. Bruce reminded him of a wiry guy he tried to block playing flag football, and the guy popped Scotty, smashed into him like a pony, and lights flashed for a second, like Scotty had stood up too fast, and everything was spinning.

Bruce was telling of firefighting. You'd come to the right city if you wanted to be a fireman. San Francisco's layout made it a pyromaniac's dream, ideal for an epic conflagration: wooden houses built squashed together like boxes. If one catches fire, they all burst into flame, right in a row. The heat drew him, Bruce said, the struggle against a primordial element. People complained about the noise of the fire engines, not him. He loved the macho trucks, adrenaline surge, axes, pry bars, big chrome nozzles, pike poles to pull down a ceiling in a controlled collapse: the smoke, the heat, the confusion.

Noah led them across the plaza. Despite a chill breeze, students sprawled on the grass, a textbook, notepad, yellow highlighter. Head askew, a blonde lay belly-down, bikini strings loosened, her whole back freckled. Pull, somebody hollered. A frisbee skidded along the air then landed, slithering in the grass. The blonde assumed a statue-like mermaid's pose, legs folded under, while her arm twisted behind her back: the play of the muscles made upside-down wedge-shaped wrinkles on either side of her back and tiny poke-marks indented the skin above her tidy waist. Noah and Bruce ambled along a diagonal path, but Scotty walked backwards watching the blonde stand and walk away, in no particular hurry to get anywhere.

Scotty refocused his attention on Bruce and Noah. Bruce was winding up some story. "Cozy," he said. "The telltale word, the dead giveaway."

"Cozy," Noah said. "Oh, I know 'cozy.' Lots of experience with 'cozy.' My whole life is 'cozy.' No need to tell me about 'cozy.' People line up for hours for 'cozy.' Know it well."

They had reached the edge of campus. Bruce squatted and adjusted and tied one of the straps of his Birkenstock sandals. He resumed the story after he stood up, telling about his present location: a single-room flat in the Western Addition, down a short alley, no longer than half a block. At night, he saw cars parked with people lying inside. He'd painted the walls white to match the ceiling but no light came in for the paint to reflect.

"Nothing but darkness," he said, "the tenant upstairs gets all the sun."

"That's the best," Noah said.

"Oh, yeah, totally," Scotty said. "The finest."

"The optimum," Noah said.

"Absolutely superlative," Bruce said. Then they all laughed at their knowingness.

Noah drove a gearshift Pinto he'd painted by hand. Angled in a space between two cars parked straight, its rear bumper sat half an inch away from touching a pole mounted with a reflective sign that said "Reserved for Customers: Violators will be Towed." Noah hauled the driver's side door out, dinging the car alongside him, and jerked the lock knob to open the passenger side door. The car shuddered as Bruce, slight as he was, crouched into the back seat. The whole passenger side dumped down, sagging, when Scotty crawled in the seat. Then the car tipped the other way as Noah slid in behind the wheel and leveled out. The interior smelled of turpentine and paint. A roll of masking tape circled the gearshift. Behind the driver's seat a suit of overalls hung from a hook. Bruce complained about stepping on brushes. A splotched tray nestled in a haphazardly folded tarp, with an angular hook-like roller on a pole sticking out.

Noah jabbed the key into the ignition and waggled the gearshift. He eased in the clutch then twisted the key one notch. The engine lights came on and then he switched the key back in the ignition. Stooped, an old lady hobbled along the pavement, dragging a tote-cart. She looked at them then pointed at the sign. When Noah waved, the lady wheeled herself and the cart around in a wide looping turn, and Scotty watched her hesitating and precarious granny walk.

"We're in a bind," Noah said after a moment.

He lived with Iris in a one-bedroom apartment near a fire station. The sirens blare so loud, you expect a ladder at the window. You walk in the front door. On the left, a narrow alcove turns into a kitchen with a linoleum floor. On the right, a door opens on a bedroom with a single window. You look down an airshaft. Windows line the far wall of the living room. They offer a splendid view of other people's backyards. And the apartment cost six-fifty a month. Noah adjusted the rearview mirror.

"And people tell me my rent is low. 'What a deal,' they say."

He notched the shifter into first. They wanted to move closer to campus. A person needed calm to study. They weren't at West Valley anymore; SF State was a real four-year university.

Noah jammed the gearshift into second: "Besides, think of the parties."

He and Iris had given their notice. They looked. When they spotted a sign for an open house, they went to the showing. They collected application sheets. They considered leasing a house. Noah had connections. He knew people. He had renovated properties, chipping blistered paint, sanding woodwork smooth, painting eight-foot walls. He held up his palm. Feel the calluses, he said. He knew an owner whose house stood empty:

the property taxes were ruining the guy. The man fretted like a father about who would marry his daughter. The place was theirs: they only had to say the word. But they needed a fourth person.

"We couldn't find anybody, not a living soul, but we were thinking of you, and then we found you."

Scotty swiveled his head, half-nodding yes, then half-shaking no, as he realized what Noah meant.

"I don't know. I had something else in mind."

Noah toyed with the gearshift. "You'd have to look tough. Walk the walk, and talk the talk. The stress would wear on you."

A minute passed. Nobody talked. A tow-truck yammered along the lane in front. Noah turned to Scotty. His hopeless eyes begged for help.

"Consider the plan. We four share a place: no apartment, no flat but a freestanding two-story house on a good-sized parcel of land. Nobody lives on top, nobody lives below, nobody lives next door. Next door is space. Unpack your records. Crank the volume as loud as you want. Save on rent: fifty bucks a month, maybe more. Fifty bucks buys a lot of beer."

"No doubt," Scotty said.

"Time is running out. Today is the deadline."

"Strictly speaking," Bruce said, "incorrect. But it is getting close. It's looming. We can afford no more postponements."

"Can we count on you?" Noah said.

"Yeah," Bruce said. "I'm stoked, are you stoked?"

"I guess I can see the house."

"It's humongous: three bedrooms, kitchen, dining room, walk-in pantry, the basement so roomy it has a washer and dryer. Even an ironing board."

"All right," Scotty said, "sounds good, let's take a look, but no promises."

"Now you're talking."

"Correct," Bruce said. "Now you *are* talking."

The tow-truck jerked back then steered towards them. Noah switched the key. The engine turned over, sputtering, coughing. The tailpipe belched and the car smelled like mulch, sweet fermented corn. The car heaved its weight forward. The steering wheel spun as Noah mashed the gas pedal. The car skidded and stalled. He notched the shifter and popped the clutch, the tires squealed for a split-second.

"You made the blacktop cry," Bruce said. "That's the best."

Noah jammed the shifter into second. With both hands, Bruce was flipping the middle finger at the truck. They were zooming along the perimeter of the lot. Spindly light poles flickered past.

"Are we clear?"

"I think so."

"We made it."

"That's the best."

"It totally is."

They picked up Noah's girlfriend, Iris, on their way to view the house. Noah told them to look for a specific fence; he had told them all about the fence. It wasn't the stereotypical fence from an old-timey movie. No, this fence was a solid wall of six-foot-tall planks, constructed tightly together. Noah knew. He hand-painted the thing with gallons of paint the color of a rusty red pumpkin. Scotty saw no such fence. Wherever he looked, he saw the houses that lived in his bedroom window "poster." So-called California bungalows assembled in well-behaved rows. Every fifty feet or so, a house number was stenciled on the curb. Scotty would then see a pebbledash walkway to the front door of said house, which split the lawn into twin patches of grass each the size of a ping-pong table. An oblong bay window sat atop the single-car garage. Each porch hid behind an iron grille and a potted cactus plant huddled on the banister.

"I tried New York, tried Los Angeles," Iris was saying. "Everything went wrong: jobs fell through, I got ticketed for jaywalking. No. I crossed on red. I walked against a red light, and this cop pulls up beside me on a motorcycle. Tickets me. Ten dollars. I pay it then I get another ticket in the mail. Disregard if you have already paid. So I throw it away. Then a warrant for my arrest comes. I take my receipt. Turns out my ticket got entered twice."

She rested her elbow on the emergency brake. They were rounding a corner.

"I didn't know what but I knew something was wrong, this feeling I had. I came to San Francisco and it was kismet, fate, destiny. Here I was meant to be, I knew, and I immediately planned to stay forever and never leave."

Noah eased off the gas, braked and swung the wobbling hatchback into a sliding stop.

"Do you feel that way?" Iris asked Scotty.

Scotty shrugged. "I guess so. I mean, I used to think so. I suppose I still do."

Noah reared up on the emergency brake. They had found the fence. Seamless, clay-colored, the planks stood as high as Noah had said, even leaning out at the top as if heading into a wind. From street-level, seated in the car, Scotty barely saw the house. The roof was slanted. The tiles, terra cotta lengths of half-pipe, scrambled to keep from falling off. Thin smoke weaved faintly upward like a bent piece of wire from a stovepipe chimney.

"Where's the landlord?"

"He's here already, inside. I know his habits. Application's probably half-filled out."

The gate rustled and cracked open, its hinges whistling. Flagstones nudged up through the grass. These flat craggy rocks were uncovered, eroded sections of the path. The house stood fifty feet back from the road and sat scalene on its slab foundation. A palm tree rubbed against the tapioca stucco exterior. Two rapier blades crisscrossed each other in an ultramarine hoop on the outside of the wall. They looked like an embossment in a book.

"What do you think?" Noah said.

"This is the weirdest thought," Scotty said. "It looks like an Edward Hopper painting."

"Maybe," Bruce said. "As to that, I don't know." He scratched his head. "Is that good?"

At the top of the steps, they used the knocker, and it clacked in the bleak light. The door swung wide and a man with a bucket-shaped head appeared. He hunched over when he walked, his level scalp gleaming in the dim porch light. He looked like a person who had lost a third of his total body weight by crash-dieting. Noah introduced the home-owner as Mr. McLachlan, who paused then shook hands with Scotty, then made for Bruce. Then Mr. McLachlan knelt on the ground and gestured for them to join him and they all sat on the grass with him.

"The lawn takes a lot of upkeep," Mr. McLachlan explained. "But people pay twice anywhere else for a patch half as big."

He got to his feet. They all stood. Mr. McLachlan ambled along the path.

"This house basically sells itself," he said. He was peeking through the branches and twigs of an untidy hedge but when Scotty came closer, he saw the inch-long thorns of a rose bush.

"No need for me to launch into any lengthy spiel or sales pitch," the landlord said quietly. They all stood there. He seemed to be dredging his mind for the right words to say, as if he feared misstating something.

"People let things slide," he said after a minute. He rubbed his eyebrow vigorously. "They walk around in high heels, dings and divots in the hardwood floors. Dust collects, the yard dries out. They run the fireplace but never clean the flue. Smell the roses but never prune the bush."

He flinched, having pricked his thumb, and he sucked the blood.

"I built this place," the landlord said, taking them on a tour of the outside of the house. "I'm not talking metaphorically or figuratively. I literally built this house from the ground up. No. From below the ground up: I poured the foundation, shoveling the concrete into the molds. I even scooped the earth out with a digger. About the only things I didn't do were survey the plot and actually draw the blueprint."

Then Mr. McLachlan climbed the steps and fiddled with the knocker: a miniature figure outfitted in a kilt, wearing a tall hat, and cradling a set of bagpipes. He pinched the figure's toes and lifted the whole body up. The knocker squeaked like a hole-punch. The landlord seemed to be peering up under the kilt. Then he slammed the feet down on the strike-pad with a sharp clack like a flat heavy drop of rain on metal.

"Friends heckled me: 'a Scottish doorknocker on a Spanish-style house?' We never planned the motifs. They happened spontaneously. We dubbed the place La Hacienda Caledonia: the Scottish Villa."

As he squinted, he scraped at the knocker with his thumbnail. "Needs a stiff wire-brush," he muttered to himself. "Ocean air greens metal. Smell the salt?"

Mr. McLachlan nudged the door then paused. For a minute, he stood, shaking his head.

"You young people go in. I can wait out here. The place needs none of my words."

Scotty nudged the door. The edge snagged the linoleum flooring then shuddered as it swung in, and he crossed the threshold. The entry led through the kitchen with a walk-in pantry that opened onto the dining room. Scotty paced the kitchen, counting fifteen creaking steps from the sink to the bay window in the dining room. Through the window Scotty could see lines of fences that partitioned the lawns of the neighboring homes into neat backyards. He looked at the built-in bookshelves that scaled the wall. The bookshelves looked like the real frame of the house.

There was a window seat in the corner near an oversized fireplace that occupied the middle of the wall. A person could sit in the window seat, Scotty thought, and stay toasty, snuggling with a novel and a cup of Earl Grey. The group hailed Scotty from upstairs, their footsteps thudding the floor overhead. He went upstairs and found Bruce capering about the room.

"What's he doing?' Scotty asked.

"Dancing: Bruce is a silent dancer. That's how he dances. But when you put real music on, he hardly twitches." Noah cuddled Iris. "It means he really likes the place."

Noah tugged Iris into the master suite and Scotty stepped into junior bedroom. He brooded. You could see why nobody wanted the room. The floor was strewn with dust bunnies and spin-devils. Straw-colored boxes piled waist-high in the middle of the floor, squares of bulging cardboard. The ceiling looked low, off-kilter. Outside the window Scotty could see fog banked in heaps like white fleeces. He could see the VA hospital, which looked like a chip of vanilla in the silvery sky. Scotty peeled open a box: a crocheted owl perched on a real branch, a child's drawings in crayon, a clock radio with a sticker of C-3PO affixed to the housing.

Back outside, the landlord was hoarsely whispering. "I want to find good tenants, somebody who appreciates the fixtures, takes proper care of the place, that's all."

Noah and Iris expressed their interest. Bruce stuck his thumbs in his armpits and flapped his elbows. They looked at Scotty. He could see himself sweep and mop the room, cart out boxes, and set his jar of stones from the beach on the wall-shelf. He saw his new "poster": a window of the city. He began nodding his head, then mouthed the words: count me in. Iris beamed so broadly her eyes wrinkled shut. Bruce pranced around. Noah gripped Scotty's shoulder.

"Rent is twelve-hundred," Mr. McLachlan said, "per month to lease. To move in, I want first and last month's rent. If you break the lease, you still pay the rent. I hold what you give me as a security deposit."

Scotty barely listened. This was happening, he could settle in at last, maybe this was his luck and fate lining up, and with almost time to spare.

"I'll follow up on your refs," the landlord said. "I should get back to you by the middle of the week. He telephoned a few days later. Everything had checked out. He would give them a shot. When could they meet him to sign the lease?

A fire smoldered. Bruce raked the embers with a poker. Noah uncorked a bottle of cheap red wine for them to celebrate with, and it spurted out onto the floor. Then he poured the wine into white ceramic coffee mugs with chipped brims. Scotty drank the wine; it tasted like flavor-burst gum to him, with a molten center of smoky chocolate and leafy raspberry.

Scotty stared at the light fixture on the ceiling in the dining room. Only one light bulb burned behind the frosted glass. In the kitchen, Iris pounded a boneless chicken breast with an aluminum tenderizer. Then she rolled the poultry in flour and drizzled oil over it and washed her hands. A pot on the burner contained steamed tomatoes and she stewed the pulp with garlic and coarse-grain salt and spread the mashed tomato paste over stiff-looking noodles on oversize dishes.

She cooked enough for all of them to eat two helpings. They ate with seriousness. When Noah spattered sauce on his shirt, he tugged it off, and sat bare-chested, twirling the noodles around his fork. They stacked the plates in the sink. They opened a pack of clove cigarettes and Noah pinched the butt tight between his thumb and middle finger, cupping the cigarette behind his palm. They passed the cigarette around, each dragging fiercely, till they'd gummed the filter up and when they smoked it, they made faces because it crackled and tasted bad. Smoke slipped out of Noah's nose, eddying around his face. Iris took another hit and stretched. Noah puffed out his chest and pumped his arms.

"Anyone for beer?"

"Why don't you kick in a few bucks?"

"Get some Weinhards."

Noah held out his palm. Bruce fished out two bills. Scotty handed over a five. They wandered down deserted, misty streets until they found a neon-lighted corner market that sat within earshot of the ocean's waves. They bought two six-packs of bottled beer and a tub of vanilla ice cream with chocolate-covered peanuts. The power lines droned above them as they walked back to their new home.

They dumped ice into a cooler and wedged the bottles inside, leaving a few out to drink right away. Noah and Bruce argued and debated political issues, military affairs and the government. Noah peeled the foil from his bottle. Governor Deukmejian gutted student grants but hiked tuition and fees every semester. Bruce nodded, but his face said, I don't care. A conspiracy, Noah growled: they kept young people stupid so they made misinformed choices. The same old status-quo politicians stayed in power. They cut funding and nobody but rich kids went to college anymore, while the uneducated and ignorant masses of their generation trained for nothing more than McJobs. They were doing nothing. Wrinkly-neck politicians! They could not let them get away with it. The time for action was now.

Scotty said nothing. He played the silent guy in the corner, watching everybody else. He started swaying on his haunches, fingers drumming his chin. He tore a napkin to pieces. Noah stoked the fire, moved a log, raking embers, until flames tittered behind the screen. Iris appeared transfixed at how the sparks flew up, bright as embers, bright as stars, then tumbled down as sooty flakes of ash. She giggled, arms crossed under her breasts, hugging herself.

Echo and the Bunnymen played on the stereo: "Bring on the Dancing Horses." The bass lines tumbled softly, like steps you could climb in the middle of the air with your heart. The song became theirs. Iris grooved to the music. Noah played air-guitar with a squiggly-veined, lumpy-knuckled fist. Scotty sang inaudibly, barely moving his mouth. His lips burbled, like he was blowing a bubble, but no bubble appeared even when he thought one should pop out at any second. Iris bent over him and messed up his hair.

"I don't know you," she said, "but I want to."

Iris and Scotty sat together listening to the music.

Scotty's foot twitched, and he dreamed about this house. I found where I'm supposed to be. He was staying forever, and he would never forget this moment, here with these people, these good people. He liked them, unlike most of the people he met. He didn't like anybody, and usually nobody liked him. But you have to give people credit. You can't write them all off. Care for them. Stop hurting. Stop. Be nice. Act friendly. You're all likeable. Everybody is, if you look. His head was sounding like the moral of a kindergartener's book. The beer washed down his throat.

Eventually, they climbed the stairs, exploring their new digs. They went into Scotty's room and saw the boxes. These are not my boxes, Scotty was saying. They're just full of odds and ends, junk, the flotsam and jetsam of somebody's life. They hauled down a box and ransacked the contents. Comic books. Baseball cards. An unopened package of party balloons and squirt guns. They filled the toy guns and balloons with water. They lobbed the balloons and shot each other. They howled with laughter. Scotty ran after Bruce, squeezing off spurts of cold water. They took the fun outside and scared a desperate-looking band of raccoons, who climbed over the fence as fast as possible. They played tag on the yard. Shrieking, yelling, hooting, then somebody somewhere slammed a door shut with a resounding crack of disapproval.

Then everyone fell silent. Something had happened. Scotty came running, stumbling, skidding along the ground to the rose bush. Iris was facing away. Noah's hand was clamped over his mouth. Bruce's lips whistled.

"You stupid ass," Noah said.

"I didn't do anything," Bruce said.

"What were you thinking?"

"We were all playing."

"You caused it."

"Nobody caused it."

Iris stood there, her hands held out, fingertips covered with chocolate syrup. Scotty edged closer to Iris and saw her face. It looked like someone had drawn crisscrossing lines on her cheeks with a dark red ballpoint. The lines were clean and neat, they reminded Scotty of the pre-surgery markings of a plastic surgeon before an operation. Iris touched her cheeks, smearing the blood from the cuts.

"What happened?" Scotty asked after a minute.

Iris tried to explain.

"It was my fault, I was standing right there, and forgot all about the rose bush, and then Bruce came, and I turned and right away I felt the branches. I thought, oh, I've made a blunder. My face felt warm, and I looked at you, and you were staring at me."

They hustled her indoors and took her straight to the bathroom.

Noah called the hospital.

"The thorns stabbed her cheeks and sliced the skin open like razors."

He cupped the handset and looked up.

"How deep are the cuts?"

"I don't know."

Bruce was tending to her, telling her to wash her face. Scotty relayed the question about the cuts.

"The cuts look clean, superficial," Bruce said. "The

thorns were sharp. It looks bad, doesn't it? But I think the injuries look worse than they actually are." He chuckled. "You look like you got in a fight with a dog." He smiled. "Or tried to break up a fight with a dog."

Nobody laughed.

"Will she need stitches?"

"I doubt it," Bruce said. "No, I'm sure. I can take care of this. No need for a trip to the emergency room."

"You're drunk," Noah said, aggressively.

"We're all drunk," Bruce answered." Want to go for a drive in the fog while drunk?"

"But what about stitches?" Noah asked. "Does she need stitches?"

"No stitches," Bruce said. He turned to Iris. "Tell me, when was your last tetanus shot?"

She told him she thought she'd had one a year ago, from when she stepped on a nail.

Bruce dug out anti-bacterial ointment from his belongings, along with a roll of gauze and surgical tape. As he applied the ointment to Iris's face, he told everybody a story.

"This guy did a header through a windshield and skimmed along the asphalt. Particles embedded in his skin. We called him 'Scraps.' The impurities scar you. This stuff will keep the wounds clean. It'll float out the junk. Nobody will know. Wrinkles, creases, folded skin. I wouldn't worry."

After patching Iris up the group sat in the living room. Bruce had ovaled open the tub of ice cream and stabbed a spoon inside, scooping out a mound of vanilla. He put the lump in his mouth. He handed the carton to Scotty, who pulled a chocolate-covered peanut loose, and bit down on it with his front teeth.

"No prospecting," Bruce instructed Scotty, "just eat what you get." He then passed the carton to Iris. It buckled in her hands. She ate a timid spoonful then offered the ice cream to Noah.

"Melted," he said. Noah tossed the carton and it spun across the room, spattering Bruce. For a second, Noah froze. A frown crumpled Bruce's face, his brow beetled. Then mouth set, he whipped the container straight at Noah and caught him in the face, and Noah flinched.

"You want to do this?" Noah said.

"Seems you do," Bruce said. He unfolded his legs and stumped along the floor for a second, then stood up awkwardly.

The two squared off like adolescents on a playground. Noah swung his right. Bruce swatted the hand down then jabbed with his left. Snapping, his knuckles tagged Noah's chin. Noah flailed his arms. He grabbed Bruce in a hug and they crashed down. It was peculiar how Iris reacted. Motionless, she watched the boys swinging their arms. They breathed in gulps, gasping. Somehow Scotty wrenched them apart. They were bruised and bloody.

"You're out," Noah said. "You're gone. No more."

"You can't just kick him out," Scotty said. He was trembling slightly.

"Whose name's on the lease?" Noah said.

Outside, an engine labored, digging up the hill in low gear. It sounded like a bus.

"I have no grief with you," Noah said to Scotty. "You can stay."

"But what about Bruce?" Scotty said. "Come on, you guys…"

"I'm not staying," Bruce said.

Scotty surprised himself a little when he said: "Then I'm going too." The words came out kind of doubtfully.

"You don't have to," Bruce said.

"Guys," Iris said. "We moved in yesterday. This is stupid. There's no need."

"It's been building up," Noah said. "They watch you. I saw them. Then they eat the food you cook."

"Can you calm down for once?" Iris said to Noah.

Noah huffed and shrugged.

Bruce ran upstairs and slammed the door. Scotty's doubts slipped away. When he turned to go, Iris grabbed his wrist.

"Wait, can we talk?"

"No. I think you should go too."

Iris drew a sharp breath. "Are you really leaving?" She looked at him strangely, as if he'd let her down.

"I'm sorry," Scotty said, "but yeah, I don't think we can stay." He looked at the ointment seeping through the gauze on her face. "It's just, well, I don't know. I hope you get better soon." He called to Noah. "No hard feelings. Really, I wish you both all the best."

"Just get out of here already," Noah said. He lighted a cigarette and pasted the stub to his lower lip. "Who cares what you do. Leave. Go."

So Scotty went, making his own way.

DONORS

Randy had a part-time philosophical mind. He thought abstractly about the future, and worried about whether he had a place in it. Here we are, he'd ponder, pretending that anything matters. But he also fretted about the present: young, broke, and solitary, he begrudged seeing people spend money (or flirt or kiss in public), maliciously rubbing it in that they had cash (and ass) on hand. At City College, he stood with the nameless students beside the concession truck as the vendor broke open a roll of quarters for her money-changer. He watched the lady sell her scorched coffee, the sugar-high doughnuts, and the moldy muffins, saw her smirk as the kids kept coming up, these slackers with tangled hair and slung backpacks.

Randy peeled off his baseball cap. In the sun, the material looked washed out, the black faded to rusty brown, like sludge on a dipstick, and the monogram's threading worked loose, unstitching the team's initials.

He sat slumped on the bench at the edge of the quad, he lit a cigarette and took a drag, inhaling a cloud of smoke. He chased the tobacco with a swig of hot coffee. He saw Pete pour a coffee and grab a glazed doughnut, then with his cheeks bulging, Pete headed for Randy while he consumed the doughnut. Randy swallowed and held his breath. Weightless, his brain went giddy in the zero-gravity of his head. Pete had a newspaper folded under his elbow as he moseyed across the quad, doing his "peezo" walk: chunky legs waddling, elbows wide from his body, like Popeye.

"Give me a small taste," Pete said, sitting down with a thump. He splayed his thick knees.

"You out again?" Randy hunkered over the cigarette, like a child guarding a toy.

"Stop bogarting," Pete said.

"I'm running low."

"I need nicotine," Pete said. "Look." His hands trembled. "I'm jittery: serious withdrawal symptoms."

"I thought you gave it up for real."

"I quit all the time. Need to give *that* up."

Randy exhaled. Smoke flowed over the brim of the paper cup. Randy and Pete both took up smoking on purpose. Smoking said: you don't want to mess with me, I don't care. People left you alone.

"Maybe I should quit," Randy said. "Or cut down. The cost kills the fun."

"You sure?" Pete said. "After a day, your lungs heave up the gunk. Something is squashing your chest, like a cement block."

Randy eased out the hard pack of American Spirits and banged the top of the box on the bench, then flicked open the flip-top. Four measly cigarettes huddled in a corner. Randy picked out a cigarette for Pete, who waved away the lighter. He only used matches. Randy watched the match head squirt into flame. Pete puffed greedily, making a flash in the air. The way Pete smoked he looked like somebody kissing his own hand.

"This roach coach," Pete said, pointing at the food truck where he and Randy bought breakfast, "is cash-money." He tapped the ashes. "No degree required. She probably never graduated high school: GED, maybe." The cigarette hung in his mouth, the filter stuck to his lip. "Minting money," he said. "Price-gouging." He ranted. "They waive tuition then ream you on snacks."

"Nobody forces us to buy her stuff," Randy said. "We do this to ourselves."

The cigarette wagged wetly in the corner of Pete's mouth as he spoke. "They use psychology," he said. "I buy coffee for a buck twenty-five. I fork over two dollars. What? Turns out a doughnut costs seventy-five cents. Help yourself. Sure. Don't mind if I do."

Randy took a mellow drag. Pete talked as much to himself as to anybody else, a rambling stream of incoherence. Pete adjusted the band of his wristwatch, muttering about how the beeper told time down to the second, and that he was sick of school. He could work with his hands. He didn't mind manual labor. He could swing a hammer like anybody.

"Who am I kidding?" Pete said. "I hate work. It's totally bugged."

"I hate even looking for work."

"What's more fucked up, once you land the job,

you have to turn around and do the job," Pete declared.

Randy chuckled involuntarily, huffing and coughing, choking on saliva.

"Think about the jobs out there," Pete said, standing up and pacing, like he was a lawyer talking to a jury. "What do you want to do? Work at Mickey D's? People trip, man, ask for stupid stuff: a cheeseburger minus the meat. A grilled-cheese sandwich? No. A cheeseburger without the burger. I actually heard somebody place this order."

Pete was clutching the paper, reading the classifieds on the back.

"Customer service: no. Telemarketer: no. Bike messenger: I don't know. You have to smack cars with your hand so they know where you are, yawp. But a bus will flatten you. I heard about a guy. Totally mangled, squished like road-kill, and the bike, barely dinged up at all. Still rideable."

Randy puffed on the cigarette. He saw himself working the counter, totting up his share of the tips at the end of the shift. Granny spoiled him: cards and letters with fives and tens. Once during a visit, he pilfered a handful of singles when his granny walked in. I was looking for something, I found this money. She waved her hand and said you can have the money now or when we're dead.

Pete stared at his wristwatch while he curled his bicep, humming a melody. Randy remembered the trick. To keep from being tardy, Pete set his watch's timer continuously every hour. Under Randy's chin, he thrust the watch like a steel compass on a silicone strap, with hash marks in place of numerals.

"And now—"

The watch beeped twice.

"—it's history time." Pete sang: "Ride captain ride, upon your *history* ship."

"Randy?" Prof. Blevins coughed harshly into his fist, swallowing a lump then chokingly whispered the name again, his finger scratching the page in the roster. The professor's scalp was tinged green from the fluorescent light in the classroom. I am not my name, Randy thought. Everybody called him Randy. Hey, Randy, a guy said, in a dopey kind of way. Somewhere a girl's voice fluted, pitch rising, his name a question. Ear cocked, he waited. Nobody said anything. Behind him somewhere, a kid giggled spitefully. They said his name wrong, mispronouncing it intentionally: sometimes he was called a drawled "Run-Dee," a choppy "Ron-Die," pompous "Ranne-duh." At 23, he felt too old to still be called Randy. Even if Prof. Blevins used the name. Call me RJ, he told him. It never caught on. A week later he became Randolph, then Randolph Jordan, then Randy again. It was what you called a twelve-year old. He wanted to holler: I am not a little kid.

Randy felt that nobody wanted to have anything to do with him. Not their cliques, coteries, or klatches. The twerps staked out the back row, the math wizards and English majors came in early to take over the front. The Cambodians, Filipinos, Sri Lankans blockaded the corner. The Chinese lined the second and third rows. A couple black kids sat near a smattering of Hispanics. Randy didn't identify with any of them, not even the generic white guys like himself. He belonged with the misfits, not cool, not uncool, treading the knife's edge between goofball and fuckup. Where a genuine doofus flunked outright with a straight F, he'd get a B minus or a C plus. He cracked the books. He studied. Notecards stacked inside a shoebox; textbook with pages highlighted in glowing yellow. I choke on exams, but I know, I know I know.

Prof. Blevins opened his briefcase and papers cascaded out of the pigskin satchel. Behind him hung a lopsided clock and he took it down from the wall, then unbuttoned his chalk-dusted blazer. Like a method actor, he worked himself up, adopted a doting, scholarly air, to tell his sad tales about dead kings. The class was his baby: the full-year Western Civilization survey course. Blevins billed the class as Neanderthals to Nazis. Students loved his shtick, the way Blevins gave historical details that were nowhere in the text, a book that cost forty bucks, even secondhand. Blevins locked his fingers, as if to pray, then he raised his forehead and started lecturing, twirling his thumbs as he talked in a melodious sing-song, with parts done in a dramatic tenor, and jokes in a deadpan monotone. Blevins rehearsed a story about ancient skeletons buried in an embrace, with metal hoops, thick as wedding bands, ringing the bones of their fingers.

Randy took off his baseball cap. Prof. Blevins made you think. A sign in his office read "tu dois changer ta vie," Randy knew the words but wondered why they needed saying. No kidding, he thought. Sometimes he pictured himself as an old man, on his deathbed, surrounded by loved ones. See you on the other side, he thought. Randy felt his life was passing him by. He envisioned himself as a TV character: an actor with a cameo, a doctor on a soap opera who delivered bad news: sorry, no treatment, terminal. I never feel like myself, he thought. He crossed off days on his calendar, and time inched forward, another day waiting to be crossed off. What would be his legacy, how did he fit into a version of history?

Blevins had switched topics, telling the class that for a time fashionable Roman ladies used eggs in their hair like gel and combed their tresses into stiff piles atop their heads. The overhead projector displayed a marble face, mound of curls, with blank eyes, on the wall. Roman proto-punk, Blevins told the class and then went on to explain that the Romans painted these statues, antiquity was gaudy. Blevins's voice squeaked, piped, whistled as he worked himself up. The Italic peninsula depopulated and Rome began to recruit centurion posts from Dalmatia and then from barbaric tribes from the North. He furrowed his brow at this development. They even had draft dodgers, he explained, men who chopped off their thumbs to make holding a sword impossible. Blevins shook his head.

"Decadence," Blevins said. "All right, the egg hair gel was a symptom, not a cause of the end of Roman civilization." He stopped, he seemed to be arguing with himself. "Right," he said, "nobody's saying that gelled hair *causes* the decline of a civilization, as in made it happen. But the new style was indicative of a change in the traditional Roman aesthetic: they were forgetting who they were. By the time we get to the Byzantines, the emperors behaved like pharaohs, oriental despots: subjects prostrated themselves and flopped on the floor as proof of reverence." Feet planted shoulder-width, he flapped his arms. "Abasement," Blevins said then stood hushed for a moment, he looked ready to say more, but then sighed.

"Go easy with the hair gel, that's what I wanted to say, unless you want to end up looking like me."

When nobody laughed, the professor's face blanched and his fingers quivered. For some reason, Randy saw Blevins sitting alone at a table, correcting papers, oblivious to an oblivious world. Nobody paid him any attention, laughing at his passion for history, which to them amounted to little more than a pile of rocks. Blevins lived in his head and it looked awfully lonely to Randy. Prof. Blevins buttoned his pitiful jacket and collected the stack of graded midterm exams. The whole room groaned. Out of shape, Blevins lumbered between the desks, incapable of speed. He had an uncanny ability to remember where his students sat and efficiently handed out the papers. As he approached Randy's seat, Blevins snorted.

"Oh, Randy," he called out, "you certainly tossed your pebble into the ocean with this one."

The room was emptying fast, the kids limped out as soon they checked their paper, but Blevins stayed at Randy's desk, preventing him from leaving. When Blevins finally moved on, Randy waited a few seconds before he peeked at his grade: seventy-eight percent, another C-plus. But he had studied. The paper was covered in a rain of red ink. He'd really blown the essay. But Blevins's behavior was downright barbaric, calling him out like that. Vicious, he thought, for a college class. Blevins had reached the place where Pete sat, and he berated Pete in a booming voice, literally tossing the paper at him:

"Congratulations: another F. If I gave this test to a chimpanzee, he'd get a higher score."

"Fucking asshole," Pete was saying. "The guy is deranged. We're only college students."

Pete and Randy were walking across campus. Along the path, students walked in pairs or alone. A squad of football players in dingy white uniforms and battered white helmets, ran tire drills, they looked like they were trying to run through a flood without getting their feet wet. They grunted loudly, their plastic helmets cracked together, their cleats tearing up patches of sod.

"How bad did you screw up?" Pete asked Randy.

"I'm still passing," Randy answered.

"I figured. I call you the history channel: you channel history."

Randy threw his head back in a parody of mirth. Pete waved his finger.

"No, all I'm saying, you have a head for the trivia. You should go see him during office hours," Pete said.

"I did already," Randy replied. "Told him I'm not a great writer. Takes me forever to write an essay. And he says, 'think of me. You write one, I read fifty.'"

"That was a shitty thing to say," Pete said. "Why did I let you talk me into this class?"

"I heard Blevins was tough but fair and writes strong recommendations for you when you want to transfer out of this dump."

"He seems like a jerk to me. The problem with

teachers like Blevins is that they make everything seem like fun and games. They crack jokes, work in wry commentary, then slam you with a ridiculously difficult midterm. Really?"

Pete stopped talking and whacked Randy's thigh with the paper then rolled it into a telescope. "Ahoy," he said.

A hippie chick strolled along the path wearing a clingy silk-screened dress, with black tights, and thong flip-flop sandals on her feet. She swished her hips as she walked. Her dirty blond dreadlocks grazed her naked tanned shoulders.

"Get it, daddy," Randy said under his breath.

"See them, they're called child-bearing hips," Pete whispered. He made a circle with his hands. "You could hold her right around the tummy."

"I'm getting hot," Randy said.

"A case of the horn," Pete said and howled through his curled up newspaper, while Randy blew into cupped hands. "Tu-doo, tu-doo," went the sound.

When Randy and Pete made cat-calls, the girl's face twitched. Randy knew her, sort of, her name was Amber and they rode the same train to college. He always inventoried the people in the car, and she was in his tally. She watched you with eyes like rain in bright sunshine. Her irises shimmered like mirrors. Randy wondered if Amber viewed the world through a silver haze. Did she see him? Sometimes he caught her looking at him and then she would quickly avert her eyes and stare straight ahead.

"See," Pete said. "She smiled at me."

"No. Neither of us fazed her."

"She winked at me."

"Involuntary," Randy said, "a reflex."

"I think she likes me," Pete said confidently.

"Keep dreaming."

Pete shrugged, turned, walked backwards, and then faced forward again.

"She's granola to the bone. Wearing the hippie-dippy clothes, sandals. I bet she's a vegetarian. Driving the Volkswagen Cabriolet. Probably has a Grateful Dead sticker in the window, you know, the skull or the dancing bears. Do you like the Grateful Dead?"

"I hate the Grateful Dead."

For a minute, they walked in silence. Then Pete talked about Amber again, disagreeing with himself. Pete took her side in his internal debate, talking her up, saying how he wanted to make her his girlfriend; then Pete berated her, taking her down a peg or two, saying that she was a tease.

"She wants guys to go gaga, stare at her. 'Want me,' she says without saying anything."

Pete's watch beeped and they jogged down the sidewalk, ducking under the chain-link fence on the overpass bridge. The whole street shuddered from the weight of a Muni metro car.

"Besides," Pete said, "a chick like her costs money. You take her out. You spend twenty bucks here, twenty bucks there. You know what you get? Nada: not a damn thing. You buy her drinks and she drinks them and thanks you at the end of evening. Then you go home alone and eat ramen noodles for a month."

"You sound disgruntled," Randy said. His feet scuffed the pavement.

"I guess. Maybe. I don't know."

The station was like a quarry with a roof: gray walls, cavernous. Wind whooshed up from the lowest level. They pounded feet, slotted their fast-passes through the turnstyle and hopped down the steps towards the train platform. An electronic board flashed "Richmond."

They got on the train and sat facing backwards. Staring at the paper, Pete smacked the back page.

"Listen," he said. "I've found a job for you. 'Sperm donors wanted. All ethnicities, ages eighteen to thirty-five. Earn up to forty dollars per visit.' Damn, man. That's good money."

"They put the same ad in there every week," Randy said. He'd never scrutinized the blurb's fine print.

"Forty bucks," Pete said. "You jerk off anyway, why not get paid? You ever do that shit at work? That's getting paid for it."

The doors of the train opened and shut at the next stop. Nobody jumped inside. Pete wadded the paper.

"What am I thinking? You're a busy boy, you'd have none left. If only they made house calls."

As they pulled into another stop Randy saw Amber. She was skipping, gingerly ascending the stairs. Randy wished: look back at me. Pete pumped his hand up and down, as if stabbing his thigh.

"Pick me, pick me, I'll do it. You don't even need to pay me. This one's on me, get it?"

An old woman got on the train and sat down, looking at Randy.

"Yeah," Randy said, "what about you? You wanna be a donor?"

Pete expelled a breath and flapped his lips.

"Aw, they'd have to pump the nurse's stomach to get mine."

In his apartment, Randy heard a child playing below the window. Randy pried apart the metal slats of the venetian blinds and peeked down at the kid. The boy booted a deflated soccer ball across the courtyard, ran after it, then kicked the ball back the way he'd come. Sometimes the ball bonged against a window cover, rattling the metal. A woman dressed for winter, belted overcoat, woolen socks, black clogs, a headscarf knotted under her chin, pegged a white undershirt to the clothesline. She shouted at the boy in a guttural language that Randy didn't recognize. Randy knew the husband, who worked at the corner market, he was always dressed in a white apron with pink stains. He called Randy "babyface," and joshed him about smoking. Why you smoke cigarette? You know is bad for you, the woman's husband would say in broken English. Make a problem, he said, pointing at Randy's crotch, then coughed a laugh. Randy watched the man's wife pick up the laundry basket. The boy peeled a piece of leather from the ball as his mother eased down on a stool. She put a hand in the small of her back, and she patted her stomach with the other hand. Randy could sense her relief. He wondered if what her husband said was true, would smoking inhibit his ability to have kids? Did he want kids? The woman was always in the building somewhere, or just outside the building, as far as Randy knew she never left. When the phone rang, he bounded and hungrily reached for the handset.

"Oh, daddy," the voice said.

"I'm busy," Randy said.

"I saw the girl from campus."

"I saw her too. We both saw her, when we were riding the train."

"I mean I saw her without any clothes on, naked."

"Sure you did."

"Seriously, she works down on Market. You know the place."

"No way."

"Oh yeah."

In his head Randy saw the street. For a joke, Randy went inside one day, after loitering outside for fifteen minutes. He never knew why but the whole time he was in the peep show he felt queasy. The rooms smelled of bleach. Inside, a dollar made the curtain rise and in the room a tattooed chubby pranced prissily on high heels, then knelt and rubbed the glass with her hand. Then the screen whirred shut. When Randy slotted another dollar, the girl bucked like a horse, hindquarters smacking the window.

"And get this," Pete was saying, "she has a scar under her belly button."

"From a caesarian?"

"I think so. It was horizontal."

"What are you going to do when she recognizes you?" Randy asked.

"She never came close enough to my window."

"Wave the money, that brings them over."

"I waited, bided my time. I never said a word. I left. Next day, when I see her on campus, I'm like, hey, hi, like we go way back, and I know all about her."

Pete talked to hear himself talk. He told all about Amber. She had moved down from Oregon, and she wrote poetry. She lived in the Mission, off Sixteenth Street, and said she waitressed at a café.

"I told her, I said, I know the area. So she says, want to get a beer? Sure, I say. She says, how about the Albion? Yeah, I say, famous place, everybody knows the Albion. She's there every Friday night. Eight o'clock? Works fine by me, I say. The Albion. Friday. Eight. I'm there. So there. So totally there."

"What are you telling me for?"

"She asked about you."

"Right."

"Listen. With a chick like her, you have to move fast. Or else she'll think, this guy, he doesn't know what he's doing."

Randy cupped the mouthpiece. He knew the routine: scam. You tag along, Pete bums smokes, sticks you with the tab. Then he brags about getting some of her, in detail.

"I'll save you seconds on her."

"Whatever."

"Just messing with you, what do I always say? Girls come and go but my little peezo-buddy is forever."

"I'm totally strapped for cash."

"I can spring for a beer. I invite, I pay. I can get some money."

"All right, let me think."

Randy put the phone back in the cradle. Show-off, he thought, Pete liked rubbing it in. Unbelievable. Money, cash. He could get money too. Randy parted the blinds: the courtyard stood empty. Who am I fooling? An interview or two, with no tangible prospects. He tried an employment agency: (psycho) Pathways. They queried him about his salary requirements. Eight dollars an hour Randy told them. Randy applied for a job at a hotel, the hotel manager told him the pay was six dollars an hour. I need seven, Randy said, I made six last year. I can't offer you the position, the manager replied. Managers and employment agency staff asked him the same questions: what do you hope to be doing in ten years? Twenty? Thirty? No clue. He visited the job center but you had to major in biology or chemistry for the jobs they had because the jobs were like internships at labs or clinics. He answered an ad for making pizza dough, temporary: the regular had broken his arm in the mixer. At a housecleaning service, the owner rested her army boots on her desk and told him that her motorcycle was leaking oil. That's a Harley for you, she said. The cleaning staff had rules against rooting through people's stuff, she said, uncrossing her ankles, but everybody does.

"You can tell yourself no, but alone you give in to the urge. You happen on strange things. Not talking about your standard freak-show masks, you know, with zippered leather. I can handle that. One time, I'm cleaning this guy's closet, and he has boxes of latex gloves, stacked from the floor to the ceiling. Okay, whatever. But here's the thing. The stack keeps going down, but I never see a single used glove in the trash can or anywhere."

"Yeah," Randy muttered then crossed the service off the list: blank that blankety-blank, he thought.

Randy never seriously considered the sperm bank, but he cut out the ad, circling the number. Easy money, he thought. He picked up his hat, undid the stubby snaps, then popped them in again. He sat, brooding, and put the hat on his head so that it slanted sideways. The brim scratched the nape of his neck when he swung his head. He dialed the number of the sperm bank. A young woman answered and had a childish voice. She asked if she could help him, and he offered his full name: Randolph Jordan. He spelled out his address and gave his phone number.

"Could you repeat your name?" she said. "I started yesterday, still getting used to this job."

The girl told Randy about the rules and requirements of sperm donation. She spoke very slowly. Sometimes she mispronounced words and then corrected herself. They rejected (first she said "ejected") roughly ninety percent of applicants due to smoking or alcohol use, he would be tested for drugs, and diseases. Then she asked him a host of personal questions. How many partners had he been with? Any venereal diseases? When was his last AIDS test? When was the last time he, she hemmed, you know, masticated? As for his sperm, the sample would be tested to determine their speed and viability. All of this information would be confidential. The law forbade the disclosure of his identity until his child reached the age of eighteen. Randy could decide then if he wanted to have contact with the child.

"It's a big decision," she said, "most people commit for a fear, I mean, a year."

"I'm okay with that," Randy said. "I have the time,

I can commit. When is your next opening?"

"We usually send you the medical and legal forms for you to fill out before you come in."

"No slots this week?"

"We're booked. Wait, I have a late opening on Friday. Three o'clock. Sometimes we get backed up. It can take longer than you think."

"Put me in."

"It's only for the sample, but I'll send you the paperwork today."

"Do I bring you the sample?"

"Oh no," she said. "We have a private room on site. We give you a cup."

"What if there's, well, a delay?"

"A delay? Oh, I understand. There are magazines, if you need help, maybe tapes. Wait." She hollered: "hey, do we have tapes?"

Somewhere in the room a nasally voice said, "Yeah, we got tapes."

She came back on the line: "There are tapes too. You go to the room by yourself and just do whatever you need to do. We send the sample to the lab."

A few days later, Randy walked towards the train station, on his way to the sperm bank, and saw a crowd of commuters standing by the fare gate, waiting a moment for their cards to be accepted before descending the stairs to the train platform. Randy rode the escalator down, staring at a wall with evenly-spaced decorative bumps. He reached the platform as the train roared into the station. The lead car stirred up ancient bits of cellophane wrappers and paper receipts, making them swirl around the rails in the tunnel. The train moved like a mechanical shark, with brushed steel skin, and the conductor's window had that dead-eyed look of a predator. When the train stopped, the conductor opened his window and peered out at the little school of humans waiting to board his train, then the doors shuttered open with a moan.

Randy boarded the train and noticed it was mostly empty, he could choose any seat he wanted. He walked indecisively down the aisle. Randy sat, then stood up, and sat down again a few times before settling in a forward-facing seat by the window. A gangly man with an untrimmed beard and a straw hat boarded the train, followed by a woman yawning, her hair getting stuck in her mouth. Plucking a lock of hair, she crossed her eyes, squinting at the ends. The train continued its journey, descending under the bay, causing Randy's ears to pop. Randy opened and closed his mouth until his ears normalized. They were beneath the bay. The train became dark, the tunnel going on and on, the train's wheels squeaking, and the car tilted. When the train ascended from the depths of the bay, Randy's ears tingled again, and he heard a faint humming or buzzing. The train was flooded with daylight. Randy looked back at the concrete tunnel as the train rode up the elevated rails. Randy took in the sights, such as they were. A steel crane pulling metal containers from a ship, train yards, spurs of tracks zippered the ground, meshed teeth, depot tanks like push-down knobs, warehouses with shabby rooftops. The rows of two-story houses looked like toys. The train swept past a postal depot, with black windows and beige stone panels. Randy knew a mailman once. The guy always wore a light blue shirt, dark blue shorts, white tube socks, and a brimless leather cap. The postman wore a sparkling stud in one earlobe. When he delivered the mail, he would tell Randy that being a postman was good work. But the rash of shootings in post offices in recent years made Randy skeptical about working for the post office. "Going postal," they called it. What kind of life was that, not for him, no thank you.

When he got to his stop, Randy stepped off the train and lit a cigarette and wandered to the end of the platform. He could see the university from where he was standing. The lecture halls became minuscule white boxes from this distance, the campus clocktower a small stick. Commuters passed Randy, eyeing him, staring. Nothing to see here, move along folks. Never mind me. He knew where he was: Oaktown.

Crouched outside the train station exit, a workman wearing a painter's mask and a bright orange vest dunked his fist into a bucket then clenched his hand tight on a sponge. The man is removing graffiti, Randy thought. Once he'd watched a fat kid with frizzy hair take out a huge marker and write "Kram" on a window. Who knew what he meant. Graffiti was timeless. In Pompeii someone had scrawled "you lap girls' privates against the city wall like a dog." Randy looked at the sperm donor clinic's paperwork and glanced down at the return address on the envelope. For some reason, the sheets came color-coded but they made no sense to him: baby blue for the tests, faded pink for the commitment, goldenrod for the payments, and sea green for the clinic's cover letter. When Randy got closer to the address on the envelope he couldn't find the building. He went back the way he'd come to see if he'd missed it. He finally found the building number where the clinic should have been but instead saw a dilapidated apartment building. No sign announced the sperm bank or even a clinic of any kind. He stood in front of it for a while but nobody entered or exited the building. He wondered if the door worked. For all he knew, maybe somebody had nailed the thing shut.

Randy peered up at the building and a child of seven or eight looked down at him from the second-floor window. Why are you not in school? Randy wondered. Probably playing hooky, skiving off, as a professor in England might say. They stared at each other and Randy waved hesitantly at the kid, who gave no reaction. Then Randy shrugged, holding up his hands: nothing. He marched around in a little circle. The kid never laughed. He never moved. Randy took off his cap and left it on the sidewalk, he gestured at it. He scooped the cap up and tossed it; the band caught in the fence. When Randy looked back, the kid flipped the bird, a stubby little middle finger. The kid made a face and mouthed swear words: "fuck you." As if flipping Randy the bird hadn't already telecast what the kid thought of him.

Little brat, Randy thought. He looked over at his hat, fluttering on the fence. Out of the corner of his eye, he saw the kid, pointing, and hollering obscenities, then an arm gathered the boy and the curtains closed up the window. A cloud blocked the sun, shadow-dark temperature drop. A church bell tolled and Randy started to laugh. What was he thinking anyhow? The things people will do when they need money. He decided to walk to the campus, crumpling up the paperwork from the clinic and threw it into a garbage can. The wad grazed the rim, noiselessly bounced off, then dropped.

"Fuggit," Randy said as the papers scattered on sidewalk. He left them as proof he came.

From the seat at the bar, Randy saw every table. There was no sign of Pete or Amber. There were other couples hunched together, murmuring in the gloom over pints of beer. Randy thumped the cigarette pack against the bar counter and shook a cigarette loose. He took long slow sips of beer while he waited for Pete. His stomach clutched his insides and they rumbled, from anxiety. The booze fizzed right up to his head. He ordered another round and drank three beers, and smoked seven cigarettes, their smoldering corpses left in the ashtray. They're not coming, he thought. He didn't even know why he'd come.

He sat with his elbows on the counter, flipping an unlit cigarette. The cigarette lighter sparked but never flamed, it was running out of fuel. He clicked the wheel three times until the flame guttered weakly, just enough to light his eighth cigarette. Except for a pocket of coins, he was broke, back to normal. And then Randy saw Pete standing by a table in the front window. He was not alone, he was seating Amber at the table. Randy slid off his bar stool, the alcohol he'd been drinking hit him like a wave, and his eyes watered. Randy stopped and watched Pete and Amber for a moment. They sat squeezed close together, giggling, then Pete glanced up at Randy. Both of them were silent. Then Pete lightened up visibly, body relaxing, and he smiled at Randy.

"Hey, glad you came. Pull up a chair, cop a squat."

Pete waved at the waitress while Randy teetered over to Pete's table. The waitress was svelte, and wore a plaid skirt with a black frilly top. From the cloth-lined pocket of his wallet, Pete pulled out a twenty-dollar bill and put it on the table. Randy struggled to understand; thoughts stampeded through his mind: disgraceful, unbelievable. Ranting internally, all Randy could think was what a sneaky bastard, and backstabber, Pete was. Randy could visualize their future together, and the vision brought some solace. They marry. Pete drops out, drives a delivery truck. She gets knocked up. Surprise: twins. Riding a kneeling bus, they unfold the baby buggy. The whores, Randy thought, fucking cheaters: they deserve each other. But Randy wondered would he ride the same bus with them? In his mind's eye, he saw himself disembarking from the bus and watching the bus leave, passing him by. A hand slapped his back.

"You all right?" Pete asked.

Randy shrugged his arm. "Yeah, go easy. Lay off."

He was staring at the waitress's unlaced boots. Her tights were torn at the knees.

"Make it three," Pete said. "Don't worry. It's on me, I'm flush."

Randy stuffed that last cigarette in his face but then on second thought he stamped the thing out. He was done with smoking.

LAKONIKOS

"**S**o this is Cal," the girl said to Stan, "and I, a simple teenager from Iran, am here."

They sat at a table in the shade of a flowering pear tree, its branches strung with light bulbs. A river of undergraduates passed them, as if the whole campus was on the move. They'd been talking for a while, but still didn't know each other's name.

"Looks like Chemistry," Stan said, gesturing at the textbook on the table. A yellow orb illuminated the book's cover. "I dropped the class after a day."

A vein decorated the side of the girl's neck, a faded tattoo of a grapevine. She tipped her acne-speckled chin up, and nodded.

"What's your major?" Stan said. He brushed a cookie crumb from the table.

"It's like you're asking me what I want to be when I grow up."

The girl began dipping the tea bag in her mug. She

removed the tea bag with a spoon and wrapped the string around the tea bag to squeeze out the water into the mug.

Stan picked at the loose strip of laminate on the table. The girl ripped open four packets of sugar and poured their contents into her tea, then she added some milk, which sank into the cup and then billowed and clouded the surface of the tea.

"You make me curious," Stan said. "I see you reading on this Friday night, and I think, it's early to dive headlong into course readings."

"A doctor of dentistry," the girl answered. She sipped, a noiseless slurp, and then gulped daintily: "an oral and maxillofacial surgeon, to be precise." After a moment, she set the cup on the saucer. "I want to fix birth defects, like harelip, or perform reconstructive surgery for the maimed, not become rich exploiting people's vanity."

She crossed a leg over her knee and rotated her foot. The cuff of her slacks uncovered a ribbon of skin and a furrow made by her flexed calf muscle. Stan had to say something because the longer he sat beside her, the more nervous he became. His fear latched his mouth shut and occasionally, when stressed or flustered, Stan stuttered or, as his family liked to say, he got his "mords wixed."

At last, he said, "it's very admirable, a lofty goal," cleanly pronouncing each syllable.

"I feel as if I was born to do it, I'm totally serious."

When she spoke, she sounded like any California girl down the block, but with a surprisingly deep voice for someone so slight. "What about you?" she asked.

"I like art, sculpture, music, literature." No stutter, but he felt like his mouth was moving in slow motion.

"You major in art?"

"No, I dabble. Babble." He laughed nervously. "I take courses in art history, music theory, but I do English, unfortunately. I tried everything else."

He felt put on the spot. It was his fault: when he asked her about her goals, he inadvertently invited her to ask him the same question.

"Psychology," she said.

"Come again?"

"My major is Psychology. For dental school, any degree is fine, as long as you take care of the science courses. Naturally, most people choose Biology or Chemistry but I have this friend who majored in Philosophy and he plans to become a cardiologist."

"I never knew," Stan replied.

Stan watched the extension of the girl's throat as she discussed her class's lab section. Then Stan's eyes descended to the buttons of her blouse, and when he looked further down his gaze lingered on the seam of her slacks. Her everything got to him, the total ensemble of western clothes, eastern appearance: the shah-girl next door. Should I ask her out on a date? The word scraped oddly in his ears. Berkeley people never dated; they hung out; they studied together; they took in a movie or bought dollar-pints at the micro-brewery. The times when he managed to stay awake, he often got lucky by default, like his one-night stand with Kassy; they had become a weekly thing there for a while. It meant nothing to Stan. But a date was daunting: what could he do on a date, where could you go? He didn't even have a car. He walked everywhere, rode the bus, or took the train. A date was highly unlikely if not outright unfeasible. Yet here this Iranian girl sat, with him. A kind of date.

Stan met the girl an hour before their "date." He wasn't looking for anybody, wasn't even trying; if he was trying anything, he was avoiding Kassy, who studied and hung out at a coffee shop in Sather Lane. Stan wore sneakers, wrinkled cargo pants, like everybody, he was incognito. After his class ended he roamed the campus aimlessly. He thought about walking home to pick up his mail, which arrived at three o'clock, but it was a long walk. Stan didn't pay attention to the protests in Sproul Plaza. He ignored the tables set up by various campus groups. They gave away flyers protesting fee hikes, made chalk drawings on the concrete, and collected paper cups for a recycling program. In the background, a middle-aged shaman in street clothes was yelling about religion.

"Where are the Protestants," he asked. His voice carried through the plaza, an amplified whisper. "Where are the Roman Catholics, where are the Jews?" The old man gulped a lungful of air: "Sky-father!"

Through the crowd, Stan saw this outlandish girl maneuver her backpack through the maze of students. Straight, ink-black, glossy hair with light olive skin. She stopped a few feet away from Stan and glanced at him with green eyes. She smiled, looked away, then peeked at him, as if to say, I saw you checking me out. He looked at her and wondered, are you looking at me? She responded, I am looking at you checking me out. He wanted to say something self-deprecating and witty, but nothing came out. So he stood, staring abashedly at her, while she looked him up and down.

A heckler was jeering the shaman. The man's face hardened into an enamel mask. He crossed his arms; speaking under his breath, mouthing an imprecation. The onlookers advanced. When the street kids stopped pounding their buckets, he bellowed, "Earth-mother," drawing out the last syllable, straining, his face red. His ferocity drove the people back. As soon as his cry stopped, the kids banged the buckets again.

"What is this guy anyway," the girl said: "what does he want?"

"I don't think he's a Jew for Jesus, at any rate."

"He's carrying *Thus Spake Zarathustra*."

Stan shrugged. "Then a Zoroastrian, maybe? This is Berserkeley. It's why we're here: free speech, free love. All part of life's rich pageant."

They stood, not speaking. I said something wrong, Stan thought, something that should have made her laugh. Berkeley could be so tediously "right-on." It didn't matter what class it was, his professors liked to tell him everything is equal, everything is culturally relative, everybody is biased: everybody has their own truth. Stan came for this challenge, and so did everybody he knew. They all felt miserable for it.

The shaman had knelt down in his beige chinos and spread his hands wide. He opened his eyes and mouth. He seemed to look right at the girl.

"Maybe he's..." Stan tapped his temple with his finger. "Berkeley's got them all. Nudists, nature-lovers, tree-huggers. And pagans, witches, wizards, alchemists. They celebrate the solstices. Saturnalia, Lupercalia."

"I think we should respect people like him."

"I sounded judgmental. I'm not like that. I guess I feel discombobulated. Who am I to talk?"

"You're being weird on me. Don't act weird, I don't like it. Everybody is acting weird on me." The girl stifled a sneeze. In the process, she dropped a pair of keys. Stooping, Stan grabbed them.

"Thanks, it's my car key," the girl said.

"What's the other key for, your house?"

"No," she said, grinning. She punched his arm. "It's the trunk key, it pops the trunk. If I lost my car keys, you'd never get in my house; you'd only get into my trunk. I don't care if you get in my trunk. There's nothing in there."

They walked to the end of the plaza. To Stan's surprise, the girl said: "Escort me to my car? I need to get something."

The girl drove a white, weather-beaten station wagon. She was parked under the tennis courts. It was the last car he would have expected to see her drive; he could barely imagine anybody so petite maneuvering this behemoth around the parking lot's pillars. She unlocked the tailgate and dumped her unwieldy backpack inside, removing the Chemistry textbook.

"You don't have a trunk."

She clutched the text flat to her chest: "whatever it is, you know."

"It's a tailgate."

"What's the difference?"

"You lift a trunk, they open upwards, but you drop a tailgate: they go down."

The car's license plate read: "Hi Maint."

As they sat now in the outdoor seating area, the girl told Stan about Iran. She was born in Isfahan, and when she was two her family escaped the country a few years before the revolution. She barely knew any Farsi. Her family planned to settle somewhere in Europe, staying in Hamburg, Germany for 18 months. On holiday, they toured London and rode the tube system, and the girl remembered the red double-decker buses, and had a photograph of herself standing beside a bobby. Even she stared when an elderly English lady scolded a queue-jumper in no uncertain terms. It was so different from Iran. During a trip to California, the girl said, her family decided to relocate for the climate. Each morning, they took tea on the patio of their house in Pleasanton, talking about events in the news.

When the Iranian Revolution began in earnest, her family was shocked by the image of men in white shirts and gray slacks smashing bottles of wine in front of a hotel. The US embassy compound was stormed, and Americans were taken hostage and blindfolded. Bearded men in turbans poked cadavers with sticks. The news made the stone-age look civilized in comparison: the streets of Tehran swarmed with shouting men punching the air. Crowds prostrated themselves in the road. On his news program, Walter Cronkite displayed a number every night to remind Americans how many days officials from the US Embassy were still in captivity.

"Our neighbor used to say," the girl said, "'one bomb would sort out the whole problem.'"

Her father trained as an architect then went into real estate in the US, while her mother became an elementary school teacher. She spoke nostalgically of returning to their homeland. Back in Iran, they lived contentedly, with a manicured garden and an apple tree; they employed a woman full-time to shop for groceries, cook, clean the house, wash the laundry. For a few dollars a day, the woman ironed every single article of clothing, undershirts, boxers, even socks. The girl remembered fondly the pleasure of starched undies and slips, crisp to the skin, unwrinkled. Probably, her mother liked to say, the clerics would leave their family alone because they always needed architects. But her father lamented the plight of girls. Old men, with a houseful of relatives and hangers-on demanding to be taken care of, married young girls and regarded them as unpaid servants: when they tapped the table, you'd better look sharp, and no griping. Had they stayed, she'd probably be married to a cleric. Here, her father encouraged her to study for a career in dental surgery.

"Persians are rightly renowned for making superb medical professionals."

"Your life sounds like an all-out adventure."

They sat in quiet for a few minutes.

"I don't know your name."

"Everybody calls me Stan."

"You don't look like a Stanley."

"No. Stavros. Sometimes people think my last name is Stavros. Stan Stavros, they say. But my last name is Grabowski. I go, unofficially, by Stan Grabs."

"I like Stavros. What does it mean?"

He made a cross with his fingers. But he didn't know what his last name meant, nobody told him. Did everybody dislike their name as he did? People asked him: are you Greek, or are you Polish? To confuse matters, the Polish side had swarthy complexions, black wavy curls; the Greek side had pale skin, reddish hair, and blue eyes. But he was only a quarter Polish and a quarter Greek; both full-blooded grandfathers had married women of mixed genes. His paternal grandmother, who married the Pole, counted herself half Irish, half German. Her family whispered of a Spaniard in their lineage. He knew little about his maternal grandmother's ancestry. Despite a connection to the Netherlands, when she married the Greek, she *became* Greek, converting to orthodoxy. Stan was baptized and nominally raised as a Catholic, the faith of his father's side. When the two clans got together they needled each other, swapping slights and calculated insults. It was complicated, he longed for simplicity. He had no feeling for his Polish or his Greek heritage. Maybe if he were one pure thing, he could give himself up to it. He envied Italians. If he were Italian, he could say, I'm Italian, even if he spoke no Italian and never set foot on Italian soil, or went to church except at Christmas and Easter. Life would be so simple.

"And you?" Stan asked. "What's your name?"

"Atoosa," the girl said. "She was the most famous queen in Persian history. It's a popular girl's name."

Stan rested his elbows on the table and interlaced his fingers. Unexpectedly, her name jogged a freshman-year memory of reading Aeschylus's *Persians* late on a Saturday night in a café. He marveled at how the playwright wrote so movingly of his mortal foe, and the pathos of Atossa's vision in which she foresees Persia's doomed invasion against the Hellenes. To praise an enemy took rhetorical skill. But those Greeks and the Romans too revered their enemies; it was an honor to beat them.

"Why do you say Persian?"

"Persian is the term for Iranians living in the diaspora. Westerners say Iranian, but when you hear the word Iran, you think of the revolution. We here call ourselves Persians."

He shook his head. "I know, I mean, I thought westerners said Persians, but Iranians said Iranian. I always thought Persian came from Latin. Parthia."

She shook her head. "The Romans and, before them, the Greeks, got the name from Parsa, the dominant kingdom. For us, Persian speaks of the greatness of the past; Iran, all that is wrong in the present time."

"That makes sense. Sorry if I offended you."

"No worries," she said. "It's a common mistake. People say Iranian all the time. But worse is being mistaken for an Arab. It's the worst insult I can imagine." She scoffed; Stan thought she might spit. "Thieving Arabs stole everything from us. They ruined our culture." She sat back. "You know, a good many of the stories in *A Thousand and One Nights* are of Persian origin."

The bell clanged, tolling in the plaza. She looked around contentedly at the gonging sound.

"You want to go somewhere else?"

She shook her head, "I should get home."

He stared at the litter of ripped sugar packets; spilled coffee ringed his napkin. He drained what was left in his paper cup. "I guess I'll see you around."

"Wait," she said. "Please walk me back to my car?"

Stan rode with Atoosa in her massive station wagon. The car smelled of hand lotion. Atoosa inserted a George Michael cassette and turned up the volume. "I want your sex" thumped in the speakers, the bass shaking the car. She mouthed the song's repetitive refrain, "I want you sex," then looked at Stan. "I'm sorry," she said. "I like the song."

For several minutes, she talked about her membership with Columbia House. Was he interested in becoming a member? She offered to give them his name and address. When she persuaded a friend to join, she received a free record.

Stan tried not to listen to the song. He stared at the roadwork outside: a trench dug in the shoulder with orange pylons.

As they neared his building Stan waved his hand in its direction. Atoosa wheeled her tank into a parking space in front of his building. They sat for a moment and she switched off the music.

"I don't believe it," she said, "you live in the green building. I drive by here, thinking, I wonder who lives here, in this green building."

"I not only live in the green building, I manage the green building. I work here. I show the units, do minor repairs and call in a contractor for major things. I touch up the paint of the green building. We use pea soup."

"Was this place a motel at one time?"

"Never. The style of the times, built in the 1960s. Floating stairs, second-floor walkways. The owners had solar panels installed to heat the water. It takes ten minutes for the shower."

Atoosa's hand grasped Stan's wrist, then she lightly swept his forearm. She squeezed his bicep and then let go. He leaned over and she shifted her weight against the armrest, reached out and shook his hand.

"When can I see you again?" Stan asked.

"This weekend is busy."

"Let me call you."

She scribbled her number. "I know you like me. I like you too. I'm not sure how much. But I go to the café every afternoon, same time as today. Meet me, we can study."

As the car lurched away, she bobbed her head and snapped her fingers. Stan took a step, then paused, and watched the car's tail lights disappear as she drove up the ramp to the freeway.

Stan and Atoosa spent time together in the following weeks. They went to cafés, to study, other times they bumped into each other purely by accident, but always in a different locale. Once Stan watched Atoosa argue with a girl about her preference for Plato over Aristotle. Stan didn't join the debate. Atoosa and the girl were taking the same class and Stan barely knew anything about philosophy. When the weather became colder Atoosa and Stan moved indoors for their study sessions. She really needed to study. The chemistry class, she said, was breaking her in half. Did he have anything to do? So Stan studied with her. They spoke intermittently. She told him about what women wrote on the partition of a stall in the women's bathroom. Stan would talk about the oddball tenants at the green building and then they would return to their books. Stan didn't really study when they were together, he mainly watched Atoosa reading. Her book splayed open, her hands leafing through the pages of color plates depicting scientific tools, mathematical equations and worms. They made an unlikely pair: an Iranian pop-music lover and a Greek-Polish apartment manager. She'd traveled the world. He'd never been outside of California. For the last two years, he doubted he'd been more than ten miles away from campus. Sitting close to her, he barely thought of her physically. But when she wasn't with him, Stan pictured her wrapping her body around his, their bodies on fire, her hair caressing his chest and shoulders, and he dreamed of her, holding her breath.

One day near midterms, when he unlocked his door, the answering machine's light blinked. Nobody called. Nobody left messages. Maybe something in the dark blocked the light, but no matter from which angle, he checked, the light was blinking. He played the message. He was surprised that Kassy called. They took the same class. At first, they sat a few seats apart in the first row. Then she ignored him and when he ignored her back she would call his name, and they would say hi awkwardly before slipping away.

"I saw you yesterday," Kassy said when Stan telephoned her back.

"You see me every day. Or used to."

"I mean, with some chick. Is she your girlfriend?"

"I only met her a few weeks ago. We hang out. We haven't been on a date."

"What's her name?"

"Atoosa."

Kassy laughed: "Medusa?"

Stan wondered now if he'd mispronounced it. The words rhymed. He spoke her name again. He even spelled the letters for Kassy.

"What kind of name is 'Atoosa'?" Kassy asked.

"There's a play by Aeschylus, called *The Persians*. The queen is Atossa."

"Persian? You mean, Iranian. You're hilarious."

Stan wrote letters to Atoosa, nothing soppy or lovey-dovey, and he became her pen-pal. He told her about a restaurant where customers sat on carpets on the floor and the waiter poured peppermint tea from three feet up in the air. A belly dancer writhed, clinking finger cymbals, and pulled male customers up to dance and took their shirts off. He told stories from his boyhood, related anecdotes about his family, described his path to Berkeley. For him, the Greek and Polish sides deserved each other. He prided himself on being thick-skinned, unflappable. You had to be, in his household when the entire extended family convened under one roof. Though he lived in the city, he rarely went home anymore. When everybody got together, the women labored in the kitchen while the men talked about property values. The meal ended, the males retired to the TV room, drinking warm Budweiser, while they flipped through the channels. All evening, they discussed sporting lore, evaluating each golfer, stock car racer, and football player who appeared on the jumbo screen.

He always wondered at being accepted by Berkeley. He was no academic superstar, and knew it.

The mother had sent him to Riordan High School but he panicked during the SAT and got a mediocre score. The lectures, the scolding: did he want to be a failure? Originally, he planned to enroll at SF State, but the family insisted on Berkeley, as a validation of all their sacrifices. He did not get in—at first. He spent three years at City College checking breadth requirements off the list for a UC-system transfer. His mother urged him to select courses on the basis of whether the class meant an easy A. She had him pester his instructors. If he received anything lower than an A-minus on a formal assignment or exam, she strongly recommended withdrawing or swapping sections: Berkeley did not accept second-best. While she hardly expected an A in every single course, she still opened every piece of official school correspondence, scrutinizing grade sheets. Then she made him explain any shortcomings.

Such were the things Stan shared with Atoosa.

Returning home, Stan hoped for a reply from Atoosa and he would scan the street for the mail truck, a white box with a reticulating cargo door, and when he saw the vehicle lurch down the street, he stared at the bank of tarnished mailboxes mounted flush in the stucco side of the building, and his eyes sought for contents in the mailbox. Most days, he made the call at thirty paces. If the box stood empty, the slits in the window grid looked like black smudges, wide as pencils. But when the box had something inside, the hatch's window grid glowed as if stuffed with a wad of gauze. Some days, he arrived while the mail carrier, wearing a pith helmet tipped back, hauled out the bank of mailboxes and stuffed the receptacles with envelopes of many hues: manila, robin's egg, lavender. Stan willed the arrival of a letter from Atoosa. When the mail carrier climbed inside the postal vehicle, Stan closed his eyes, twisted the key, then probed the corners with his fingertips. Empty-handed, or clutching a bill from PG&E, he lowered the face plate and extracted the key.

On many afternoons, the lady in an apartment on the second floor peeked down at Stan when he checked his mailbox. Stan could see her watching him, as she pretended to dust the carved-wood figures that sat on her windowsill. The little statues looked religious to him. A shepherd bore a lamb in his arms. Beside that knelt an angel, hands clasped, wings folded, like a replica of a headstone. A female figurine balanced an amphora on her head. A robed colossus of a man with a sculpted beard wielded a crosier.

"What makes you so eager to check the mail," she finally hollered at Stan, "it's too early for grades."

Then she pulled down her window shade. She rarely spoke to anyone. When her grandchildren visited her she danced with the kids in the courtyard, an old lady dance. She shuffled in a raincoat and floppy cloth hat. How could he answer her question? He could ask her why she kept saints on her sill. What did she expect, what did she hope for? Was there some religious regulation for the periodic changing of the figures, dependent on season or cycle?

The semester rolled flat like a carpet being pushed out. Stan worked hard, studying late, falling asleep with the book open and the lights on; he hauled himself close to the table, slouched over, etching the paper with strokes of ink. But he avoided the cafés where he and Atoosa used to hang out. Every day, he took alternative routes around campus. He became the opposite of a stalker, a reverse-stalker, an avoider. Whatever they had was over. Still, Stan wondered, he'd made a gallant effort. The experience with Atoosa reminded Stan of job interviews he'd aced but then never heard back from the company. Stan never believed she'd strung him along. He wondered what to say if ever he saw her again. They had been friends, hanging-out buddies, as she liked to say. One mid-November afternoon, when he passed a thrift store on Telegraph, he heard his real name being called: Stavros Grabowski. Then he saw Atoosa come out and she grabbed his arm.

"I missed you," she said, smiling.

They ended up going to their café and sat outside, in their usual spot, by the railing, beneath the bare branches of the flowering pear tree. Autumn ceded to winter, and the day ended early, the light bulbs glowed in the tree. Atoosa told Stan about a guy who said he'd call her but never did. Stan wondered if she was talking about him or about somebody else. Turned out, it was someone else, named Tucker. Atoosa was Tucker's hanging-out buddy. Tucker was infatuated with a saleswoman at a men's clothing store in the city. Tucker continually cleared his schedule for the woman but she stood him up every time. Atoosa had spoken to Tucker the previous night. And Tucker told Atoosa that the woman had a one-night stand with a guy she met at a dance club. It meant nothing, the woman told Tucker and Tucker repeated the story to Atoosa, clearly, as she understood the matter, to console himself.

"Then he tells me," Atoosa said, "'when ready to be serious, she'll come around.'" Atoosa stifled a sob. "He kicked me right in the heart."

Stan ran his fingers through his coarse tufts of hair. This Tucker-guy must be an idiot, he thought.

"Why don't you call him?" Stan said after a while.

"I don't know why I can't just pick up the phone and dial the number. I want to talk to him in person, say what I have to say directly to his face, even if he laughs at me."

The foam of the steamed milk was evaporating. She sniffled.

"It's all right," she said, squeezing her eyes shut. "I'm tough." A tear trickled down her face. "Please, a napkin, if you could."

She blotted her cheek. "So embarrassing," she said. She folded the napkin in a neat square, like a real handkerchief, as if she planned to save the napkin for later use.

Stan's family pestered him into coming home for Thanksgiving; and, against his better judgment, he went. He became Stavros Grabowski again. For the Greek side, he was all Greek. The Polish side counted him as all "polski." His family was loud, they liked to wind him up. Eventually they dragged the story of Atoosa out of him. They had fun mispronouncing her name. Somebody talked of how the Greeks beat back the Persians (as if it happened just last week). Though tiny, fractious, the Greeks defeated a mighty empire because they prized freedom more than life itself. Then one of Stan's Polish relatives said the Greeks held slaves. It was true, spoke an uncle with a white leonine head of hair, the Greeks took slaves. So did everybody. But the Greeks fought their own battles; the Persians forced slaves to fight for them.

Then the squabbling and the boasting began. Stan listened to them talking, everybody wanted to show you how wrong you were.

"But I read the Persian Empire was the world's first great multicultural experiment."

"What's so great about that?"

"I knew this Arab girl from Jordan. Always talked about how great Jordan was, as if she lived there, not here. The thing was, she drank, partied, and screwed around, but never with her own kind, because they liked to say bad things."

"I never understand: westerners have nothing to teach anybody but everything to learn from everybody else: they can do no wrong, we can do no right."

"They have this attitude, like they need to bring real culture to us, civilize us."

"They have no thought-mechanisms for self-criticism."

"I like my culture. It's mine. Also, it has the advantage of being superior."

Stan shook his head: "oh, me," he thought. No wonder he was so mixed up.

Final exams started in mid-December and were accompanied by cold stinging rain. The wind needled Stan. Unraveling clouds soaked the campus; crumpled coffee cups littered the ground by the stone trash receptacles. They silenced the clocktower. Stan entered a twilight period during his final exams, a headache that lasted for a number of disjointed days. Stan felt raw, as if his skin had been peeled off, exposing musculature and nerves to the wet and rain. When an exam ended, he felt physically drained. If he drank a liter of water, he thirsted still. Depleted, he swore he'd used his own blood to write in the answers on his exams. He battled a head cold and had a sore throat. He pushed them away in his mind. I cannot get sick. I can fall to pieces when the exams end. By the last day of exams, Stan was barely functioning, then a burst of energy kicked in and the panic attacks eased up. He trekked across campus to his last examination, grinding sodden leaves underfoot, stepping over miscellaneous puddles formed in the uneven crevices of the sidewalk slabs. He heckled the crazy old man with the bible, or as Stan called him: the "Godbother." Stan chipped a quarter in a street kid's cup. The drizzle stopped. A timid sun glinted on the puddles. The final exam period ended, and the campus's clocktower bell began to ring again.

A few days before Christmas, Stan received a message from Kassy. She had two tickets for a play in the city tonight.

"Are you asking me?" Stan said, trying to get over his surprise at hearing from her.

"No, Mr. Grabs," Kassy said. "I can't go. And nobody I know likes the theater. You're the artsy one."

"What's the title of the play?"

"*Scapin.*"

"Escaping?"

"I don't know how to pronounce it. It's some play by Molière," she said, pronouncing the name correctly.

"I'm pretty broke right now," Stan said.

"No money. They were complimentary, a shame to let the tickets go to waste. You can pick them up at the box office."

Stan told her he would like to go but everybody he knew had gone home for the break.

"There's nobody you can ask?"

He was shaking his head then said: "Not really."

"What about your Persian girl?"

"We fell out of touch."

"Call her. I'm sure she'd be glad to hear from her old buddy Stan Grabs, if nothing else."

When he cradled the receiver, the cord knotted. He unplugged the jack and let the cord relax. The address book lay open, his eye tracing the shallow cuneiform left from erasing Atoosa's name. He lifted the receiver and punched the buttons, then hung up. After resting his elbows, he dialed the number again. A man's gruff cigarette-voice answered. Before Stan could explain who he was, the man talked over him, asking Stan the reason for telephoning them. Stan gave his real name.

"Ah, Stavros, I hear that you write elegant letters."

"Can Atoosa come to the phone?"

Stan heard a hand muffle the receiver. The man called Atoosa's name. A second later, she came on the line. Something clicked: the man had hung up.

"I haven't seen you for a while," Atoosa said. Her voice sounded scratchy, as if she spoke through a veil or a handkerchief.

"I got behind," Stan said, pushing his chair back.

"Yeah? I'm already behind for spring. I wish they had carrels at Strada. I practically live there as it is."

After a moment, Stan asked Atoosa if she had any plans for the evening and told her about the tickets.

"What play?"

"Something by Molière," he said, and she accepted his invitation.

They sat in the balcony. Stan was dressed in a pair of tight-fitting brown corduroys, a white-collared shirt, and a gray sweater with fraying cuffs. Atoosa sat with her back arched, legs crossed, wearing a pink tiger-striped mini-skirt and black knee-high boots. They watched the main character make his way down the aisle towards the stage. Dressed like a hobo, he shook people's hands then climbed on the stage. During the play, when Stan tried to speak, Atoosa sealed her mouth and pointed at the stage. As the curtain came down, an actor dressed like the playwright, in wig and frilly period costume, scaled a ladder towards the balcony, as if to protest what had been done to his play. The chorus chanted the main character's name as the audience left the auditorium.

"I hope you had fun," Stan said, when they reached the lobby.

"I wished they'd stuck closer to the original."

"I guess they updated it, to make it seem relevant."

"Ever read any Molière?" She glanced down. "Oh, never mind me, a purist. The play felt more like The Three Stooges than Molière."

Stan walked Atoosa to her car, and she leaned against the side and held her hand out towards him.

"Tonight was nice," she said. "Thanks."

"It was fun," Stan said. "we should do something again sometime." Atoosa nodded and sat in her big white station wagon, then drove towards the freeway.

Stan was wiped out but he kept awaking from vivid dreams, where he found himself mouthing her name. He caught glimpses and impressions of the dreams he had: people in robes prostrate in the streets, mud-walled dwellings, a minaret tall as a smokestack, a grim wailing noise in the background. He was going to kiss her. When their lips touched, her tongue darted out through the seam of her mouth. Through the mattress he was falling and he reached out and squeezed nothing and when his eyes opened in the dark of the small hours, his hands were clutching the bed sheet.

Stan was so distracted by his silly emotions that he almost forgot about his grades. Then the mailman appeared, wearing that pith helmet. He tossed a lumpy sack into the truck and closed the cargo door and drove off. Today something is going to happen. Stan squinted through the slits in his blinds. He went to his mailbox and found something was inside. He inched the key in and twisted. A satiny black envelope, big as a greeting card, sat wedged in the box. As the blinds upstairs louvered open, Stan flipped over the black rectangle. Sent bulk rate from Terre Haute, Indiana, the envelope announced that Mr. Stan Grabs was pre-approved: welcome to Columbia House Records!

For several minutes, he clutched the envelope in confusion and then anger—at himself. The old lady from upstairs was watching him from her window sill. He tore the envelope down the middle, right across the address. He stacked the halves then ripped them into quarters. He kept ripping, tearing the papers to shreds. He started smiling at the noise the tearing paper made.

"Who's going to pick up them scraps," the old lady yelled down.

"It's just junk," Stan said then whispered: "let somebody else come and get them."

The old lady shut her blinds. Then Stan walked away from that place, with his forearm raised, shielding his eyes from the sharp-pointed rays of the dropping sun.

TRAILER

They get ready to climb inside the trailer at midnight, the sky dark as ocean-bottom, standing on a tin-colored sidewalk. The big rig's diesel engine rattles and shakes the cab, windshield and doors. These parts continue to vibrate when the motor abruptly shudders off. Countless boxes, stacked to the roof, cram fifty feet of trailer bed. The team hauls the ramp from the back of the trailer and two of them place the end on the pavement, with a scrape. In the trailer, Wade stands the dolly up. Beside him a bedraggled blond girl wrestles a box to the floor. The shiftleader's gloved hands clutch the grips and she rolls the dolly, its wheels squeaking rhythmically, down the ramp. The blond girl snaps upright and she and Wade watch the woman's ungainly stride, loose, awkward, like two tired walkers bumping into each other.

"What does she need with the dolly?" Wade says. "We should have it."

The girl hugs a box. "I guess full-timers get first dibs," she says.

"We're unloading, everything's here. It doesn't make any sense."

"Let's ask her." The box skidding to the ramp, the girl grunts then burps. "Never mind, just kidding" After a moment, she catches her breath and says, "the poor lady earns a pittance, overseeing these dudes, and she's stuck with this job."

As she grapples with another box, Wade thinks back to earlier, before they started, when he overheard the girl talking to the driver, telling him she was an art student who recently graduated from college. She didn't mean it to brag, she said, as the man tugged the fringe of beard stuck to his cheeks. If anything she was embarrassed about her course of study. Look at me, she said, gesturing at the night, here I am. The employment agency promised her clerical work, but she got manual labor instead: earlier she'd moved sofa beds. At some point the girl stood next to Wade as they waited for their next assignment. She huffed and yawned and rolled her eyes. I know so many girls like her, Wade thought then: the kind of kid who projected a frustrated air of entitlement. They had boneheaded ideas about the world as if, in their capacity as losers, they had a privileged insight into the world's machinations that was beyond the experience of the average person. They held back from trying to accomplish anything; fearful of risk, their failure became a virtue.

Wade squats, setting down the box. The cold snap has come early this year, by a more than a month. Most years, during the last week, the temperature drops into the thirties; sometimes snow falls, only to melt upon hitting the street. But right now the sky smells damp, metallic, snow in the near future. A trawler is motoring out in the bay, its wake splashing against the yacht hulls, and a forlorn clang of a buoy beyond the marina. It is the first time Wade has visited the area since the break-up with his girlfriend, a split he instigated. Wade pictures how she left, never looking back, straight into a life without him.

The girl loosens her body and cracks her neck incrementally, one vertebra at a time. She yawns unabashedly, mouth wide. A few minutes later, she tells Wade she never visits the docks, only came because here was where the job was. She pauses and rubs her nose. "You live close by?"

"No," Wade says. "Very far away: Amazon Street, in the Excelsior."

Her cheeks sag; a half-smile creases her lips. "And I thought I had a long haul."

When he says nothing back, she tells him she lives out by the zoo. She barely slept the night before. Maybe she dozed; the shade knocked against the window. How her muscles ached; she dozed then snapped awake, eyeing the number on the clock. She worried she'd miss the bus, which ran so infrequently at night, and then she'd be late. So she got out of bed and waited.

Wade never planned to work tonight, but he said yes as an excuse to take a break from his film project. He didn't come to work for the money, he didn't know he'd come to the docks. He didn't know what he was supposed to be doing. From time to time, he worked as a film extra, or he handled the lighting for an acting troupe: without pay of course. The documentary he is in theory working on will tell the story of low-wage workers in the city, like the Chinese seamstresses who ride the bus at seven in the morning to sweatshops south of Market Street. He often thought he needed firsthand experience to have material for the film short. So he did this work. But to say he liked temp work was false; nobody likes temp work. You only mind it less because the job never lasts. Everything is material, when you temp. It is field research, speaking to a question Wade has: how does a minimum wage-earner manage to make ends meet in the city? As his team resumes moving the boxes, he tries not to think about how much money the taxi ride to this job cost him. He waited for the bus, staring at a Mr. Jenkins poster, but the bus never came, so he waved down a taxi. The driver complained about passengers who didn't tip him enough. The trip burned three hours' worth of wages before Wade even punched the clock.

The girl stoops, rolls down her sock and scratches her pallid shin energetically. "You think we're getting anywhere here?"

Wade pries a box loose and eases the edge down his thigh. He peers into the rampart of cardboard boxes and sees they have cleared a sizeable area. "A quarter unloaded, I reckon: fifteen feet, maybe."

"Digging ourselves out of an avalanche would be easier," she says. A few seconds pass. "We make an all-right team," she says, "we work in tandem."

Her name is Jill something. Jill, he thinks, like the nursery rhyme. If he runs up the hill to fetch a pail of water, will she come tumbling after? The name seems so unimaginative, a little girl's name. He guesses she's about 22, but maybe as old as 30. She's slight and waiflike, with fragile bone structure, and an odd yellow tint in her hair, like a chick's fluff, right down to the scalp. She is a weird kind of pretty, he thinks. She's munching on a bar of chocolate, breaking off small pieces and nibbling them furtively. His mind dwells on her body. She looks doable enough. He pictures sleeping with her, imagining her warm and tender insides. He rakes his hair, which feels bonded to his forehead. Why are you thinking of a waste like her?

Somewhere a clock strikes two. Boxes pile up at the edge of the trailer. In the dark, the dolly appears to mount the ramp under its own volition, pulled by an invisible thread. Their shiftleader hobbles up the ramp, the same clumsy way of walking. Then she slides the carry-edge under the stacked boxes.

"How are you two holding up?" The shiftleader is looking at Wade more than at Jill.

Wade nods. "All right, I guess." He yawns and realizes how exhausted he is. Every muscle in his body is sore. He's got dust in his eyes and, when he inhales, he smells sulfur and pickles. Somewhere behind the row of shops built over the marina, a sea lion barks and yelps. Wade's mind is tired, and he has an odd dislocated sense of time: he thinks of today as yesterday, and he is not ready for tomorrow.

The shiftleader counts her steps in the trailer bed, which is scuffed and flaking.

"I knew you two would make short work of this trailer," she says upon coming back. "When I saw you, I thought to myself, they can help. They listen. They look trustworthy. Some people, they sham. But you two are squared away." Her voice seems to fizzle out. Then her face muscles relax and a half-smile twists her lips. "Thank you," she says, "it means a lot."

Jill stifles a cough. The three of them stand silently. After a moment, the shiftleader grabs the dolly's handles. "We'll take a breather as soon as we get this trailer emptied, so keep the boxes coming."

She trundles another load down the ramp.

Huffing, grunting, Wade and Jill waltz awkwardly with the boxes to the rear of the trailer. They kick them. They push them. They pull them. They coax them. They heap them in stacks. They wait for the shiftleader to dolly the loads down. Sweat soaks Wade's shirt. For much of the time, Jill talks randomly. She dislikes bright light. She likes rain and fog. She wonders why people walk so slowly. She gambles, plays the lottery. She wishes she never studied art.

"I'd sell the degree back. If they gave me the money, I'd relinquish all privileges pertaining thereto." She shakes her head. "Time. Effort. Grief. Money."

"How bad is your debt?"

"Bad, very bad. I mean, I think it's very not good."

"What like five grand?"

Jill scoffs. "I wish it were so low. That's like one semester's worth."

"Ten thousand?"

"Keep going," she says then sighs.

"Fifteen then."

"Twenty," she says, "plus change: amazing, right?"

He tells her he studies cinema at SFSU, taking

classes from Francis Ford Coppola's brother. He ran into Nicolas Cage at a bookstore once. Cage was wearing Elvis sunglasses, as he ambled down the aisle of textbooks, crooning incomprehensibly. Of course, Wade worries about how he'll make a living after graduation. Being nonchalant comes easy when you have no stake in anything serious. Soon the question will be how to make rent, pay the bills, buy groceries, everything just to survive. Compared to adult life, college is paint-by-numbers: take this class, buy this textbook, write this paper. Wade shakes his head. He is becoming skeptical about the advantages of his college degree, to phrase it mildly.

"I work, pay my way," Jill is saying. "I'm no spoiled little girl. I have no sugar-daddy."

I am somebody, she says. She does not say this frivolously, in a corny bumper-sticker way. She means that when a supervisor wants something done, they always ask *somebody* to do it, and she's that somebody. I'm the sucker they give all the work to. I type this, file that, copy these, and file those. Yes, she is definitely somebody. Somebody who spends all her time running, rushing, one gig after another. All the time thinking (hoping) the temp gig might extend into a full-time position. But she has to look sharp and take pains to make herself indispensible.

"I breathe, I live, I eat, I sleep. I'm keeping an eye out for opportunities."

Later, after a period of quiet, she asks Wade what he hopes to do.

"Anything," he says. "I can work as a projectionist. An extra."

"Do you want to act, direct, or write?"

"Everything," he says, "all of the above. I think in images more than in words."

"How are you going to ever write a screenplay?"

Before thinking much, he shakes his head. "I write: some scenes, dialogue."

She frowns. "Sounds like going about the whole thing backwards: what you are about, what do you want to say?" Then she swats his arm. "You don't need to mind me."

He shrugs: "No, they're fair points. It's my vocation. It's why I'm here, I think."

"Everybody thinks they have these aspirations. What if your vocation is impossible?"

"I want to believe it is possible, that things work out. Someday, luck catches up with you, if you wait, and your break comes. Don't you think so? I mean, I thought I was pessimistic."

Wade pauses. He doesn't know why he is saying these things, as if he believed them.

"I no longer hold such views," she says. "What I want doesn't matter. I'm no good at anything anyhow. I'd be happy as a secretary. I never grew up dreaming about it, but I need money. I need something stable, with regular hours. Doesn't this kind of scheduling kill your creativity, always scrambling?"

Wade cringes a little, worried she's calling him out. "I carry cards with me," he tells her anyway. "I'm writing an outline right now. I have a story in mind."

"Did this story actually happen?"

"Of course not, I make everything up." Wade answers. "Well, not everything."

After a moment, the girl tries to lift a box, steps clumsily; the box slips out of her grasp. The box tumbles onto the concrete floor and lands with a dull crack: shearing crockery.

"Should we tell her?" Wade asks.

"They might decide to dock our pay."

"We can say we—" He pauses. "Never mind. I'm tired as hell."

"They plan for breakage. Let's keep unloading, that's our job. Let them sort the mess."

Now when they cart boxes to the ramp, they have to walk them the whole way down the trailer. They stomp their feet, slapping the trailer's side. Wade's arms quiver as he reaches down for the last stacked box. He shoves it to the exit of the trailer. Jill gives him a high-five when he gets out of the trailer. Down on the pavement, Wade stares at the big rig's rearmost tires squashed against the curb. In the dark, the trailer looks like a square iceberg. The semi-tractor is a white cab-over with an aerodyne wind foil, and the driver's door, a square of white paint, flaps open, and the driver's boots scramble backwards down the steps and drop to the ground, the driver stretching and shaking his limbs.

"What time is it?" Wade asks the driver.

"Coming up on four," the man says. "You two worked fast. I can barely believe it. I have a free hour because of you."

For a few minutes, the driver gazes at the bridge and listens to the sound of early commuters, their car headlights twinkling on the upper deck.

"What an uncivil hour," the man says. "They must leave home at three in the morning. Suits, wheelers and dealers, bankers, stockbrokers, executives, corporate raiders. What do they actually do at those desks all day long?" He shakes his head.

At four o'clock, the shiftleader whistles to summon everybody behind the trailer. Wade watches the crew straggle in and cluster in a bunch at the ramp, standing around, talking and nodding. From her clipboard, the shiftleader hollers out names. When she doesn't get a response from one of the names she's called, she glances up and then scribbles on her notepad. When she's finished with this activity, she announces a fifteen-minute break. The temps move off, making themselves scarce. As the night sky begins to lighten, Wade roams along the pier between the buildings. Jill leans on the railing, gazing at the marina like an art connoisseur, an appraiser of pictorial perfection. The piers stretch like empty sleeves draped over the water. Yachts jostle, a faint jangle of bells. The sea lions lying together inhale and exhale noisily. Their sound is like snoring or wheezing, only louder: the collective breathing of a colony of sleepers.

A horn honks and Wade returns to the staging area. The eighteen-wheeler jerks and stammers. The semi-truck sits for a minute, the blunt cab shaking, then pulls away, making a jack-knife turn around the corner, then motors up the hill. The doors swing open on the empty trailer. The driver never shut them. When the trailer crests the hill, the shiftleader ticks names on the clipboard and gesturing at the long zigzagging lines of boxes, announces she is extending the break: she encourages her crew to get a cup of coffee or grab a bite to eat if they're hungry.

"See you back in an hour," she says.

After ten minutes, the temps enter a diner and gather round a table, the waitress hands them laminated menus. Everybody looks hungry, and Wade is beginning to feel tired again. He sits beside Jill. Someone has left the pink entertainment section from the newspaper and, while Jill puckers a coin purse, Wade reads the paper. He peeks at Jill. She stares robotically at her cup of coffee as she swirls the spoon in the mug. Jill sips her coffee as the waitress jots down their orders: a plate of waffles, eggs sunnyside up, singed bacon strips fried to black crispiness.

Jill pushes the menu away. "Nothing for me, the coffee is fine."

"We still have three or four more hours of work," Wade says. He orders pancakes and sausage links. "I can share."

"My stomach's bad." Jill says. "But you seem to be doing fine."

"Yeah," Wade says. "I was really tired, it comes in waves, but I think I'm getting my second wind."

When a lull ensues, Wade scans the listings: theater names, movies, showing times. He is making faces, snickering. She asks him why he is laughing.

"Ed Wood at the Castro," he says.

"I saw," Jill says. "He made movies dressed up in women's clothing."

"This is a movie he directed: *Plan Nine from Outer Space*. It's bad."

"So bad it's almost good?"

"No," Wade says, "just bad. Frankly bad, clunking bad, groan-inducing bad."

"You're piquing my curiosity."

She finishes her coffee and jiggles the mug at the waitress to indicate she needs more coffee. Wade asks her if she wants to see a late matinee, when they finish the work.

"You like the Castro?" Jill asks while she crushes a napkin into a wad.

"The movie theater, I do." Wade describes the antique neon sign hanging vertically in front of the theater, the mullioned windows, the Wurlitzer, the pictures of nymphs frolicking under classical pillars of a ruined agora on the wall.

"I've never been inside," Jill says.

"It's the only reason I go there at all."

"I knew all along the district is not your kind of place, not your scene at all."

"What about you, is it yours?"

"Sometimes. Every now and then. Well, used to be. Somehow never went to the theater."

When the plates arrive at their table Wade folds the pink section of the paper, then forks the stack of pancakes and cuts a wedge. He tells her he is serious about the matinee.

"We'll see," Jill says. "I want to be available this afternoon, if the agency has anything. They needed everybody to get this store ready for Friday. So the secretary told me. I prefer clerical, but the urgency."

"Yeah," Wade says. He knows. He heard her say the same thing earlier.

They rejoin the crew just as the shiftleader is calling names from the clipboard. She is skipping over people. The darkness is fading and a smidgen of sun is peeking out. In the twilight, the boxes jut out from the delivery door.

"We're backlogged," the shiftleader says, "what are we going to do about all these boxes everywhere?"

Every box will need to be put inside the storeroom before the crew does anything else. The shiftleader yells out more names. Wade never hears his or Jill's name get called.

"Only the fulltimers," Jill grumbles.

"So, everybody," the shiftleader says. "Tomorrow, eight o'clock, we stock shelves."

Jill's hands ball into fists. She stomps her feet, paces back and forth, gangly, rattling strides. I'm too tired to get angry, Wade thinks, but Jill's face has turned ruddy and splotched.

"I'm calling the office. They promised eight hours. They can't let us go so early."

"Think of me," Wade says, "with the cab fare and breakfast figured in, I barely broke even for the day."

"You should call," Jill replies, "we both need to."

"I'm wiped out, zapped."

"Really? I feel wired."

"Maybe you can snag something else for later."

She says nothing and flexes her neck.

"I thought you might take me to the movie."

"You still want to?"

"Day's a bust. I'll never sleep. Let's meet up."

Five hours later, Wade is pacing the sidewalk across from the marquee, halting every few steps to scan the sidewalk for Jill. The sun glints on the massive arched expanse of mullioned glass; he looks up at the façade of the theater. The bas-relief, niches, drooping garlands, scrolls, pediments, and bunched fronds; so much time has passed since he last watched anything here. He can't remember the name of the film. Was it the gritty neo-realist Italian movie made during the war or the French movie about the artist sketching the nude model in real-time? Wade clenches his jaw. Once, the movie theater functioned as his sanctuary with its tiled box office, hushed vestibule, the rows like pews, the chandelier on the ceiling, and the pipe organ, a stage. This was his retreat, his hermitage. He reflects on how he has never brought anyone, never let anyone in on the secret, the private place in the back row where he always sits by himself, from the previews till the last credit rolls and the house lights come on. Maybe Jill will stand me up, Wade thinks, a bit hopefully. A moment later, he spots her skulking along the store fronts. She scratches a lottery card, makes a face, then crumples the paper. Wade watches her as she tosses the wadded piece of paper in the drain.

"You sleep?" Jill asks.

"I lay down," Wade says, "closed my eyes, woke up snoring, it was more of a symbolic, fake sleep."

Wade pays for their tickets at the old ticket window; because of the glare, he can hardly see the woman inside. She wears glasses and has a bulbous chin. She hands him his tickets. The usher tears a notch in the tickets and tells them to enjoy the show.

When they go into the theater, Wade automatically sits in the last row. Jill looks at the empty seats. "Can we sit up closer to the front?"

"I like taking in the whole auditorium."

For several minutes, Wade sits, tense, holding his body away from Jill's. The bucket of popcorn in her lap smells of butter, she squeaks while she chews. The noise irritates him, and on top of that, she's hogging the armrest. The room darkens and the only light comes from the projection room. He can hear the projector shuttering. As the film plays, Wade tries to gauge Jill's interest, but her face shows nothing. Her body is stiff and prim. Then she chuckles, tittering at the inane lines of dialogue that the actors emote so melodramatically. Her legs sprawl. She slinks down, her knee splays, grazing his thigh, and his hand creeps down her waist while she rubs his zipper. On the screen, the flickering actress gazes wistfully, and when she says, "I reach over and touch it," Jill giggles.

After some time, she says, "you stop or we go."

In Jill's apartment a sachet of tea steeps in a honey jar on the kitchen counter. It looks as if some honey is left in there. Jill inspects the contents of the fridge. The top shelf holds a carton of milk, a dozen eggs, and a few cans of beer. She pops the tab on a beer and hands it to Wade. They drink and romp around the room then lie rigidly on the twin mattress. She unlaces her shoes and tugs off her socks and spreads her toes freakishly. They look like little fingers, and she kneads her swollen soles. Then she unbuttons her blouse.

"You have a fine body for film," Wade says.

"I'm a pale worm," she says while she unbuckles his belt. He studies her yellow hair. I like her, he thinks, the little waif's growing on me. She's good. He realizes he's grinning, mouth wide open. After a moment she pauses and looks up at him, prettily stretching her jaw.

"I once knew a girl who danced totally nude," she says. She bends her neck. "She raked in some loot, sixty grand last year: cash, undeclared income."

She raises the can of beer to her lips. "I watched her once," she says. "The booth stinks of bleach, but she keeps dancing in the little mirrored room, and all around men huddle in their booths, feeding her dollar bills, one after another."

"Would you want to do something like that?" Wade asks, jokingly.

She shakes her head. "It sounds hot in the abstract but not when I really think about it."

She takes the beer down and, with froth on her lip, swallows noisily. When Wade drinks his share of the beer, they touch gently on the mattress. Wade kisses her on the cheek, holding back, and for the rest of the evening they snuggle chastely. We can sleep, he thinks, I'm wiped out anyway. Her breathing becomes deep; not snoring, humming.

A mounting static, scratchy like an old vinyl record, hisses in his ears, waking him from slumber. Blaring, a voice warbles, "I reach over and touch it." The lamp pries his lids apart. Somebody is shaking him. He snaps upright. Jill stands, half-dressed, while the snippet plays again: a voice like a forties-era b-movie starlet.

"Very wooden," the deejay says. Her voice is husky, as if she's caught a cold.

A puzzled look on her face, Jill fastens the clasps of her bra. Wade is staring at the clock radio when the deejay announces the first caller to identify the movie the dialogue comes from will win a hundred dollars.

"It's from the movie we saw yesterday!" Jill shouts.

"I remember."

She grows excited, rushes for the cordless phone. When the station reads the number to call, she taps the handset's buttons.

"I can't believe it. Something I know. Never made money from something I know."

Music chimes on the radio, some seventies song with an irritating sax refrain. Suddenly, Jill tosses the phone to Wade. A man twangs, tinny, on the line. He fields the callers, he says, and asks Wade what is the name of the movie.

"I know the movie," Wade says. *"Plan Nine from Outer Space."*

The man places him on hold. Now, on the radio, the station is giving the traffic report. You can hear the throb of a helicopter's rotors. Snarls, accidents clog the 280, rubberneck-delays, congestion making the 101 a parking lot. Wade drums his fingers. The deejay runs the snippet again.

"For one hundred dollars," she says, "would you be able to tell me the movie's title."

"From Here to Eternity?"

"Sorry," the deejay says. Jill is rolling her eyes.

"On the Waterfront?"

"That's not it," the deejay says. Jill, shaking her palms, pleads with the ceiling.

"The Towering Inferno?"

"Wrong answer," the deejay says. Jill's mouthing the words, "Yeah, I'll say."

Wade alternates ears. Seven o'clock flashes on the clock. He switches off the phone.

"What are you doing?" Jill asks. She presses the redial button.

"They already named every movie."

Wade can hear the man's voice. Jill names the movie, says she has to go to work soon. The deejay milks the movie trivia gags for as long as she can, the man explains.

"Stay on the line," he says, "your turn will come."

"You hear," Jill says. "We just have to wait."

Callers name b-movies and cult films so arcane Wade snorts in disbelief. The callers keep giving the wrong answer and then the song with the annoying saxophone riff plays again. Time elapses: half an hour, forty-five minutes. At eight o'clock Wade tells Jill they need to go.

Jill covers the mouthpiece. "When I win, I'll pick you up in a taxi."

At the pier, they are setting up displays in the store. Tasmanian Devil sweatshirts hang staggered on drooping chrome bars. Bugs Bunny toys, Tweety birds, Sylvester cats populate the shelves. Wade pinches anti-theft clasps, tagging, alone, every piece of merchandise. His thumb tingles. The fleshy pad has gone numb. When this task is done, he works behind the store smashing cracked mugs and plates. In the marina the sea lions, brown as mud, loll on the docks. The lazy beasts, Wade thinks. They get riled when an interloper encroaches on the space where they sleep. Why have they let them colonize the dock? An uproar breaks out.

During the rest of the day, Wade looks for Jill. For some reason, he pictures her pacing her bedroom, phone clenched against her face, teeth grinding. When the shiftleader asks about her, Wade shrugs, as if to say, who can tell with anyone? But her absence bothers him; he even gets worried, the way you do when you think something bad might've happened to somebody close to you.

Wade's next assignment is making cold-calls for a charity. Due to a shortfall of funds, they are raffling autographed footballs. When he phones the people on the list, they say they have donated already and ask not to be called again this year. Nothing, Wade thinks, has ever tired him out more than talking to people on the phone, giving the same speech, for eight hours at a stretch. Luckily, the job lasts two days. For a week, he mans the front desk at a company. During the Christmas season, the phone barely rings and he has nothing to do and the days drag along. Wade's next assignment is to cut yellow pages from the phone book with a razor blade and then photocopy the pages on sheets of yellow paper. Eventually, he replaces the pages and returns the books to the shelves. Scratch paper and post-its ask could somebody type this whatever, copy such-and-such document, and file these papers. Wade grins while he types this, files that, copies these and files those. I guess I am that "somebody" now, he thinks. I'm the sucker they dump all the work on that nobody else will do.

From time to time, Wade wonders about Jill. She never turns up at the agency anymore, even on Fridays when the temps drop off their timecards. Once, in the lull at the end of the year, while waiting to hand in his timecard, he flips through the stack of crumpled magazines. He sees an article about radio shows and he knows the subject is going to make him upset. It is not your old-fashioned radio show anymore. What you hear at home on the radio is heard by everybody in the country. Sometime before the actual broadcast, the deejays prerecord their shows with canned requests, and syndicate the tapes to local stations around the country. What you think is being aired live might be weeks old, already broadcast by a dozen or more subsidiaries. Nobody can ever tell the difference. A technician operates the tapes, handles the phone, and splices in traffic reports, advisories, breaking news as necessary. In this way, your local station cuts costs significantly.

That very day Wade sees Jill downtown. It takes a second for the recognition to kick in. Her hair looks darker, her face is slightly tanned. Dressed in a gray jacket, cream blouse, and slacks, she walks beside a jowly man in an olive double-breasted suit. The man is shaking the ice in a plastic cup. I should tell her about the radio article, Wade thinks. But he says nothing: he really has nothing else to tell her. He can imagine her saying, it doesn't surprise me. Well, good for her.

Later Wade is standing, propped against the glass of the movie theater. He scarcely glances at the marquee. Inside, an usher slumps in a lounge chair.

"Which cinema?" the ticket seller asks through the speaker. He asks again. Wade says nothing. The seller looks ready to shoo Wade away. After a moment, the ticket seller reaches for the handset of the phone. Wade realizes he is gripping the sill. He is staring at a small rectangular placard set at an angle behind the glass, and Wade lets the meaning of the words sink into him.

> Hiring Opportunities
> Apply Within
> Start Immediately

True, he thinks, a good idea. About time, too.

That night he lies in bed not sleeping. Maybe he dozes off. His muscles ache. Suddenly Wade is gripped not so much by inspiration as by the feeling that he has to do something or he might never do anything. He gets up, grabs his Braun Super 8. He runs to the bus stop. There is the same Mr. Jenkins poster he saw that first night when he went down to the pier and met Jill. He loses track of time during the bus ride. When he reaches the pier, he walks to the deck behind the store. He sets up the camera and shoots the sea lions sprawling mud-colored against the bottle-green water on their dock spur while a trawler motors out into the bay. The boat's wake splashes water against the hulls of the yachts and sailboats. Wade keeps filming when a bull sea lion barks and sets off a whole dinning hullabaloo, still filming even after the noise gradually ebbs away.

BAIT AND TACKLE

The Richmond train sat waiting in the station for the Concord train, for the passengers connecting, due any minute now. A solitary police officer paced up and down the train platform, staring down the rails gleaming in the moonlight. The walkie-talkie on his hip crackled and hissed, a voice cut in and out. Buddy winced at the squall of static the police officer's gadget made. Buddy was waiting for the Concord train. There was no announcement about any delays but a hunch told him the Concord train was going to be late. If he needed to he could walk the street under the overhead train tracks to get home. Just follow the rails and you're safe: probably.

On a good night, he managed; he got through it; but long before the train stalled his night began turning out bad. He threw up in the toilet at work and when he flushed, the toilet bowl got clogged. Then he rolled up his sleeves and plunged the bowl. A customer walked in while he was doing this and quickly left. The plumber came to the office and Buddy watched the man snake twenty feet of steel cable into the drain in the floor and extract strings, cellophane, and rubber bands, then wind the cable and dismantle the drain-cleaning machine. The plumber told Buddy the strings caught in the pipe joints and crisscrossed, making a net for stool.

Buddy grew tired of waiting for the train and decided to walk. At first, he kept the station in sight, glancing back over his shoulder, watching the entrance recede but cautiously gauging the distance in case his connecting train somehow still arrived. He'd have to sprint back, hoping the passengers from each train dawdled across the platform. But then he was too far from the station to run back. A breeze stirred the tall grass, a shushing, lisping gust. He wiped his dry lips with the sleeve of his blazer. He was almost happy when a pedestrian clopped noisily on the other side of the street. At each corner, he lingered, peering into the narrowing darkness. The houses rose in pointed clumps with yellow-lighted porches. A dog pawed an unconvincing chain link fence, barking intermittently, as if questioning the night: who goes there?

The number one thing was not to look lost, Buddy thought. Sometimes he walked in the middle of the street and kept a steady pace. He never cut across a parking lot. He heard stories. While on an evening stroll, the manager of his apartment building got held up at gunpoint. A rumor circulated that a female grad student suffered a severe beating on this block. Nobody cared. The attacker smacked her in the face, grabbed her by the shoulders and throttled her before hitching back his fist and socking her in her mouth. The fall chipped her front teeth. She lay, whimpering, moaning. Porch lights came on. Curtains lifted. While she yelled for help, the attacker loomed over her, making no move to run away. He waved at the people staring from the windows. Nobody lifted a finger to help. Nobody dialed 9-1-1. The porch lights went dark, the curtains dropped.

As Buddy walked along he made out the sound of the train rolling into the station back behind and above him. The rails seemed to hum. And he watched the Concord train accelerate along the bend of rail overhead. A voice in his head berated him: why didn't you wait for the train? Pictures of a pleasant train ride ran though his mind: the rust-colored carpet, empty seats, the slow approach into Rockridge over the parking spaces and outside the window the big red logo of the Lucky supermarket and then his journey would be finished. But when he blinked, the overhead tracks lay bare; they were silent. He experienced a feeling of temporal distortion and spatial dislocation; he adjusted his new eyeglasses, which supposedly corrected his astigmatism. They made the ground appear closer. But he could clearly discern the houselights on the side of the hills, along with some trees and a moon so round and bright he could almost hear it move. He put his glasses back on and looked again at the skewed world.

At the corner, a taxi hopped the curb and grew bigger as it came toward him. A dimly-lit advertisement displayed a half-naked woman wearing a belly-dancer's veil. The model had smoky eyes and a ribbon choker around her throat. The taxi slowly passed him, moving dead slow, an oval face in each window, and Buddy asked himself, why is the driver puttering along? The car lunged forward, as if tripping over something, then braked, its rear-end shaking skittishly.

Buddy stood watching the taxi in disbelief. What was going on? His life flashed before his eyes. He wondered what had set this series of mishaps in motion. If only he'd left on time. If only he'd stuck with the day shift. If only he'd stayed on the train. If only this, if only that, or if only some other thing that escaped him. He thought of making a break for it, like a stunt man in a movie magically outpacing a speeding car whose tires screech on the pavement. He made his mind face the truth of the situation. It was too late to change course. My time has come, he thought: my turn for a mugging. No going back now. Then somebody hollered his name and Buddy thought: I'm hearing things. Who would be calling him?

The taxi scooted backwards, its wheels splashing a puddle of water in a clogged drain. When the car stopped, the passenger-side door cracked open, revealing three passengers. The man in the passenger seat stepped out of the vehicle, his rangy-framed body wielding the passenger-side door like a shield tipped sideways and held horizontally.

"Buddy," the man said, "is a stick-up waiting to happen." He was talking to somebody inside. His voice rumbled softly, a smooth baritone that echoed in Buddy's ears like talk in an empty room. "At this rate, one day you'll be a statistic on a police blotter."

"Wait," Buddy said. "Is that Logan?"

"Long time no talk," Logan said. He shook Buddy's hand, squeezing it so hard, that Buddy's joints cracked.

"All right," Buddy said, "I keypad with this hand. Ease up on the metacarpals."

For a few seconds, neither of them spoke. Buddy relaxed and became conscious of his heart pulsating in his chest. He was gasping. The panic dissipated like a fever breaking, seeping through his forehead and chilling the skin of his brow with clammy perspiration. No need to be so jittery; he was safe. Long ago, Logan and Buddy operated as something of a twosome. Logan would simply show up at Buddy's doorstep, phone him, or they'd rendezvous somewhere.

You never knew with Logan, he had a mystery about him. His folks owned a split-level in the city, but Logan maintained no fixed address as far as Buddy knew. Logan worked odd jobs: security at a hotel, club bouncer, night watchman. A rumor went around that he had an advanced degree in economics. In college, Logan and Buddy routinely boozed, staggering from one bar to the next, and when Logan spotted a pay phone, he unfolded a tattered sheet of yellow legal paper and dialed the numbers until somebody answered. The paper got taken out, unfolded, folded, then wedged in the wallet; half the numbers were faded, erased, or smeared. But most of the time the girls Logan called showed up and tagged along on the crawl, hanger-on types, frail, fragile, pretty enough. Sometimes they slept together in the same room, hearing everything, the guttural whispers, the sloppy sounds, and then breathing in the sweaty air. After a while, it became no fun anymore. It was just weird, bordering on creepy.

"We swung by your place," Logan was saying. "I

see the kitchen light so I call from the gas station across the street, looking at the window, and the phone keeps ringing, but nobody answers."

Buddy looked at the passengers in the car. In the back seat sat a girl with puppy-fat cheeks, lounging, twirling a tuft of hair around a pale stubby finger. Behind the driver, someone was wearing a sun-hat with a large brim.

"I pulled the swing shift today," Buddy said. "They needed me. It was a mistake. Everything went wrong."

"You need a different job," Logan said.

"I know," Buddy said, "I work all the time. Work is all I do nowadays, but I'm getting nowhere. Sometimes I feel I pulled a muscle in my head."

"Next time, go punch in then leave. Come back to clock out."

Logan looked dressed for leisure, as if he planned to play golf somewhere tonight. A dark polo-neck shirt, buttoned, with horizontal stripes spaced a few inches apart, shrink-wrapped his chest. His biceps bulged like bricks stuffed in the sleeves. The pleats of his pale trousers housed legs as big around as a regular person's waist. He had the physique of an Olympic sprinter. They walked towards the taxi, and for a few seconds, Buddy felt Logan's eyes focus on his feet then pan up to the top of his head, as if measuring him.

"What size are you?" Logan asked.

"I border on a small medium or a big small."

Logan was raising the trunk. "My supervisor is this little scrawny dude. He calls me a 'mesomorph.' So I broke his locker open."

Logan's face wrinkled, a crooked smirk; it was the

smile of people who chuckle halfheartedly because they're jaded and nothing makes them laugh outright anymore. Logan opened the trunk and took out some clothing on some hangers. They were starched long-sleeved shirts, dress slacks, and sport jackets, draped in a clingy transparent bag.

"You have a week's wardrobe here," Logan said then draped the garments over Buddy's sleeve. "Spruce yourself up, hit the pavement, find new work. You could interview in these clothes."

Logan slammed the trunk; Buddy hugged the garments; the hooks of the hangers floated down in a wheeze of plastic wrap and starch.

"We need to tie one on," Logan said, "like the old days, like we used to."

"I'm trying to get home: the train stopped for some reason. Of course, once I start walking home, the train goes by right overhead, last outbound for the night."

"Sounds like this calls for a beer. Let's get a beer, one little beer."

"Yeah, I don't know." Buddy blinked rapidly. "I thought I'd be home by now."

"All right, two beers tops. I never have more than two: before the third."

Logan gripped Buddy's shoulder. "There are two of them." He sniggered at the girl with the chubby face. "No guarantee, but she looks pretty cuddly."

Buddy pictured the girl in bed with him, surprised at the vividness of the image. He could see her resting her cheek on the sagging mattress and arching her back while her hands tightened on her hips, and he imagined her swaying backwards on her knees, relaxing against him, like a tawny cat, purring. I am vulnerable, her eyes said. I trust you. Take care not to hurt me. The image dissolved and he was staring at the striptease girl on the signboard. He tilted his head till his neck made a cracking noise.

"Where did you have in mind?" Buddy asked.

"Does it matter?" Logan shrugged. "We can go somewhere local."

For a few seconds, Buddy mulled the matter over. "Is the Bait and Tackle still open?"

"We can find out. It'll be like old times."

"All right, I suppose so."

Logan chortled, "I never guessed you would take so much arm-twisting."

While Logan directed the cabbie to the Bait and Tackle, Buddy hugged his knees in the back seat between the girls. Something aluminum rattled on the floor, a crumpled can; a stack of newspapers flapped in the draft. A few glass bottles clinked in a grocery bag.

"Never mind the clutter," the cabbie said. "I recycle but the center was closed today."

The girls with Logan came from Finland. Logan introduced Anna-Liisa, wearing the hat, and Mielikki, who told them to call her Millie. Neither seemed impressed that Buddy knew that Finland in Finnish was Suomi. With her upturned sprite's nose, Millie could pass for a teenager. She had awkward eyes that looked away quickly, and fuzzy cheeks. She had a timid handshake. Seated in the middle, Buddy squeezed her hand loosely. Anna had a svelte girlish figure with large breasts. The cord of her ridiculous hat hung beneath her bosom. She fingered the knot intently. Narrow shoulders, pale oval face; she looked plain, haggard, frail: like somebody that got sick all the time. When the car bounced over a bump, she shivered and her dress rode up, uncovering the raw, mushy knees of a hotel maid scrubbing floors all day. When the girls spoke, their words banged and popped. It made Buddy think of a Spaniard speaking English with a Russian accent: a staccato rhythm, staticky and abrasive, the result of smoking a few too many cigarettes and drinking a little too much vodka.

"Is your name real?" Anna said.

Buddy smiled, mouth closed, and nodded. The girls puffed air out then spoke in Finnish.

"But it is a nickname," Millie said once Anna's voice trailed off.

Buddy had explained the origin of his name many times; he began the recitation.

"My dad loved jazz, named me after Buddy Guy. They ribbed me at school. 'Here, boy, no, down, boy. Hey, sidekick, hey, partner.' Kids are so comic."

"In Finland," Millie said, "nobody has such a name. It might be illegal."

"He's kidding," Logan said to her.

Buddy fished in his wallet. "Check my license."

While Logan studied the laminated card, Millie shook her head; Anna gazed at Logan's fingers pinching the card's top corners, holding it up to the roof.

"It's official: Buddy."

The girls leaned forward, gaped, eyes round and wide. Anna's mouth blurted an incomprehensible salvo and at first Millie smiled weakly but then she giggled.

"I'd better keep my last name to myself," Buddy said when all the mirth at his expense subsided.

"Shall we make you say it?" Anna asked.

"Nobody ever believes me."

Anna bent forward and laid her hand on Logan's bicep, then grabbed at the license.

Logan handed the license back. "You want me to tell what it says?"

"Come on," Millie said.

"Gosh," Buddy said. My last name is 'Gosh.'"

"Oh, gosh," Logan said sarcastically.

The driver swung the taxi into a space at the Bait and Tackle. The building looked like a shed joined to an oversized doghouse. Famous for a reason Buddy never fathomed. The place had been featured in a newspaper a while back. The ramshackle structure of plank walls started as a garage that sold bait and lures before being converted into a speakeasy-like dive bar with cheap beer on tap and sawdust on the floor. Then the place expanded with an annex larger than the original shack. Nobody knew when the building actually went up. No permit existed for its construction. People believed the annex came in the fifties. Somehow the place lasted, holding on despite the odds.

Logan was bending down by the driver's window.

"Fifty dollars," he said, "no way."

"Not counting any gratuity."

Logan motioned for Buddy. "Would you accept the clothing in lieu of payment?"

Buddy was getting his first look at the cabbie. A wave of hair combed sideways, a gelled mass squished flat on the man's crown. He looked edgy, fight-ready.

"How about I pay twenty and throw in all the clothes?" Logan said.

"I can drive in gym clothes. I need no fancy attire."

For a moment, nobody said anything. The police were mentioned. Anna pouted like a model in a two-page perfume spread. She walked around the hood; headlights washed the skin of her knees, corn-silk wisps on her shins. When she unbuckled her handbag, Logan wriggled a finger. He slid the folded stack of bills from a gold money-clip and Buddy watched him hand three twenties to the cabbie.

When the driver began counting singles from a wad, Logan slipped the money clip in his pocket. "Keep your tip money."

The cabbie wedged the clump of bills in his pocket. "I don't like you," he said and drove off, the stripper girl on the signboard winked and flaunted the beaded necklace she wore.

Logan never twitched or flinched; the taxi stalled halfway down the block.

"You can walk fast and stop him."

Logan snorted. "It's a regular occurrence. Guy mouths off." Logan knuckled his palm, smacking jabs. "If I clobber him, I'm bad: pick on somebody your own size. If the guy bests me, he's the underdog taking down the odds-on favorite."

Down the block the taxi's starter played a shrill grinding song.

Logan stared through the window, shaped like a portal, on the bar's door. When he wedged his body through the swing-doors, Buddy and the girls followed him. Inside, they clumsily bunched up. Everybody staring at the guy lugging the dry-cleaning, Buddy thought. People tumbled round the square tables sitting on torn cushions with stuffing poking out. A three-bladed fan twirled listlessly in the ceiling. Familiar smells of vinegary beer, pine disinfectant, and muggy sweat permeated the room. As Logan skirted the tables, Buddy tugged the garments through the bodies. The only open space was in the back near a shuffleboard table. The board looked like a twenty-two-foot butcher's block, sprinkled with sand. At the far end, a stout man with a sweaty face tossed a coin and shook a pudgy fist in triumph. Then he asked Anna if she wanted to play.

"I don't know shuffleboard," Anna said.

Droplets of sweat beaded the man's forehead. He looked ready to start raining. "I can show you," he said, blotting his forehead with a paper napkin, and he started explaining the rules. Usually, they flipped a coin to see who would have the hammer and shoot last, but they could lay for the shot if she was willing. She stared at him with blank eyes. He showed her how to shuffle a weight along the table, shooting from the side. She watched the motion of his arm, back and forth, and the loose-boned fling of his hand. The red puck drifted along the edge of the gutter then veered towards the center. Anna never moved. She kept watching the weight, spinning on the sand until it stopped and teetered on the edge.

"Hanger," the man said. He turned to Anna. "You knock me off or I will have the hammer this game."

Buddy hung the clothes on the back edge of the jukebox. The cover was tacky from spilled beer; the record-player croaked and stuttered some Bob Dylan song about a lady. When Buddy bumped the side, the record skipped and the music trailed off.

Logan tried beckoning the woman at the taps. "Where's the waitress?"

"I didn't know they had table service," Buddy said.

"I guess we have to go up to the bar." Logan raised his voice. "What do you want?"

"Amaretto sour," Anna said.

"Same for me," Millie said.

"And potato chips," Anna said, "the salt and vinegar kind."

"None for me," Millie said. "I want nothing else."

A few minutes later, Logan returned with a pitcher, two drinks, and the chips. While Logan positioned the schooners on the jukebox, Anna tore open the bag. Lips parted, she stuck out her tongue and licked the chip, turned it over, then licked the other side. Logan forgot about pouring the beer; the pitcher hung poised in the air. Anna laid the soggy chip in a napkin. When Logan made a face, she shook the packet and ovaled the end under his chin. He wagged his head.

"Why you don't want any?"

"You're licking them."

"I like the salt and flavor but the chips are fattening."

"We can ask for a salt shaker. And vinegar."

When Anna giggled, Logan hefted the pitcher and the beer turned into a sudsy froth as he poured it into a glass. Buddy drank his beer. They drank mechanically:

swig, gulp, hiccup. Logan topped off the glasses and they drank again. They finished the glassful and poured seconds. The beer seemed to change taste as Buddy drank: sugarless iced tea, fizzy carbonated water, a sour smolder of vinegar. When Logan sloshed a third glassful from the pitcher, the girls sauntered away and joined the shuffleboard game.

For a minute, Buddy stared at the bundle of clothes hanging on the jukebox. He was avoiding looking at Millie. When he peeked, she was sipping her drink; a man lit a cigarette for her. Anna was leaning down over the table and the man gripped her wrist, whispering into the brim of her hat. Tittering, she removed it, and when she looked at Buddy, he glanced away, removed his glasses, and held the lenses up to the light.

"You look earnest," Logan said. He splashed the pitcher's dregs into the schooners. "You don't need to sound as if you're proposing."

"I'm being myself."

"I'm not saying to be somebody else. You look clean-cut, kind of stiff: predictable. When you ask a girl out, it probably seems like a chore. You have to act like it's no big deal."

"I think I'm pretty laid-back already."

Logan tipped back the schooner then twirled his finger around the brim.

"Women want a guy to take charge. Be an alpha. You act like a boy scout. They want us as badly as we want them. Remember: they're no angels." He laughed.

A table opened by the jukebox and they sat down. Cradling his chin, Logan watched the tubby man stretch his arm out. They both lifted their chins as the weight floated. It was quiet for several seconds. The weights collided tenderly with a gentle clacking.

"I'm getting this round too. Go talk to Millie."

"I doubt she cares."

"She's seeing if you'll come after her."

"She went because Anna's over there. By the way, the fat guy's going to scoop you."

Logan's face wrinkled into a halfway smile. He leaned back, jostling the wall boards, and Buddy watched him crack his knuckles.

"He's not her type. But I credit him for trying."

"He seemed witty. Girls like a funny guy. They like to be made to laugh."

"Anna's using him to get a reaction out of me."

Logan rose to his feet. Where he touched the table, his fingers daubed the surface with moist prints. Buddy watched him shrug his weight, wedging his shoulder through the crowd. He never pushed anybody; at his approach, everybody eased back. When blocked, he tapped the person's shoulder and a clearing opened. Buddy could see him at the counter. It looked like an antique writing desk fitted with levers. Perched crookedly, angled inwards, two televisions sat atop either end of the liquor shelf, tuned to the same channel: a boxing match with two worn-out bruisers hugging on the ropes, digging hopeless punches into the other's waist. For a long time, Buddy looked at the screen; his face became mellow each time the fighters clinched, due to fatigue.

The pitcher thudded down.

"Yours is a confidence problem," Logan said when

he sat back down at the table. He began filling the schooners. "You seem timid. They scent desperation. They gravitate towards strength. We like looks, a nice ass, big boobs. They like dominance, status." Smirking, he dragged his palms across his chest. "Work on your body language. Stop slouching. Never shy away from anybody. If somebody tries make you get out of their way, you stop, stand completely still, and become a lamp post. Let them move. They will."

"I can handle myself all right," Buddy said. But he quailed inwardly, stomach twisting, at the idea of being involved in a real fight.

"You're no weakling but you punch below your weight. If you let yourself get pushed around in little ways, you'll never stand up for yourself in a serious situation."

After drinking half the glass, Logan sat sullen. "Maybe it's my military training. Self-defense meant making sure the other guy stayed down."

Logan pawed Buddy's shoulder. "You ever consider taking a course in self-defense?"

Buddy shook his head.

"What about carrying a firearm?"

Buddy scowled. Maybe having a gun bolstered some people's confidence but he doubted he would have the nerve to the point a gun at somebody let alone pull the trigger.

Logan huffed in exasperation.

"No more being afraid, a little swagger strikes fear in people's hearts," Logan said. He was gazing at the round, short-stemmed glasses. "Besides, women love rough edges."

Buddy suddenly realized he was drunk. Everything was getting mixed up. Somehow, he reined in his mind and said, "We were talking about self-defense. Now we're talking about women."

"Scrapping and chasing skirt connect," Logan said. As though fiercely praying, he rubbed his hands together.

Buddy smiled peevishly. Quiet for several seconds, he fought a shiver as if a breeze crept under his clothes. "What can I say? I never know."

Most times when he saw some girl with some guy, he wondered: how can she like him when nobody likes me? What, he wondered, did these women ever see in the guys they liked? They were all stupid, and deserved each other.

Logan flexed his hand. Buddy noticed some faded bruises. Logan's eyes became vacant, and he inhaled a deep breath and exhaled, blinking his eyes, now looking like somebody trying to meditate.

"Listen, but listen. I like women a lot, all of them. Through my mind the thought passes of sleeping with them all. I speculate: what she's like; what does she do? What will she let me do to her?"

As Logan talked, Buddy sucked in his belly. When he exhaled, everything felt soggy and slack, his insides wilted from despair.

"You dominate them," Logan droned on. "Think like a conqueror, a conquistador. No joke. Either you conquer them or they conquer you. Not physically: you beat their minds. Get past their thinking. Tap into their deeper selves. Go primordial. Nothing gets a girl like knowing you can protect her physically." He leaned down and stared wearily at the table. "Some like the idea you may resort to violence on their behalf."

Logan mocked Buddy by pretending to snore. "You're a romantic. I know. I've been there myself. We all have. They take advantage of you. Nobody respects weaklings. They laugh. They laughed at me. But I came back. I stopped caring. You need to exude this aura of nonchalance. It attracts them. You'll be beating them off with a stick."

When Logan leaned forward, he lifted the pitcher. "It's an act, what they do," he said. "Some girls only understand meanness. They love complaining. Men become their project. They try to tame you, like breaking a stallion. Anna belongs to this category."

The hair on Buddy's neck stood on end. He had sifted and weighed Logan's ideas long ago. You attract, he believed, what you project. One day, he'd meet a girl and get married; but he wouldn't meet her in a place like this.

But then negative thoughts began to assail him. Somebody marry him? He couldn't summon an image of domesticity. Not very likely; he needed to try dating first. His recent bout of poor luck baffled him. Back in college, he had no trouble. So casual, why not meet for coffee, how about a beer, bring some friends. Nothing happened like that now. When he last talked to a girl, he complimented her on her hairstyle, even though it looked like somebody seized handfuls of hair and chopped at it with a straight razor. Sometimes he would try to strike up a conversation with a girl. Is that a new nose-ring? How so tanned? At this point, the girl Buddy was talking to would mention she had a boyfriend, a husband, a girlfriend. He was relieved when he talked to a girl and she never mentioned a significant other, even if she had somebody. Sometimes he got a phone number and asked them out. Usually, they said yes. But at the last minute, they'd cancel or stand him up.

Logan nudged the empty pitcher. "This is your round, my friend."

Scooting back the chair, Buddy couldn't remember how much he'd had to drink. Was this last call? For a moment, he swayed in place, worried all the alcohol he'd drunk would hit him at once. He figured he'd had the equivalent of about half a gallon of beer. He drank twice that much in college and didn't get hammered. But that wasn't the case anymore. Get hold of yourself, he said, calm down, before you do something dumb. Buddy decided to walk back step by step. Nobody moved. An elbow knocked him. When he turned, a swaying head laughed smoke in his face. Whoa, he was telling himself.

The group drank now in cheerless silence. Time became woozy; everything lagged; there were gaps when he nodded off and couldn't remember the last thing he'd said or done. Buddy watched himself pick up the schooner, tip it back, then stabilize the glass's base on the table. He was losing his thirst. There was little enjoyment. This was boozing to do damage. He was beyond his capacity. His stomach accepted the beer reluctantly, and then his esophagus blocked it from reaching his stomach anymore and he hiccupped. Logan swatted him between the shoulders and Buddy coughed. Several times, he swallowed, wincing. He hiccupped again and held his breath and then the hiccups eased and he breathed again. It made his mouth taste of stomach acid. I'm full, he thought, as he fought to swallow it back down.

In the men's room, Buddy swayed over the trough, steadied by a hand on the partition by the door. The spot offered a vantage point of the back room. He spotted a guy playing knock-off unclench a bulging leather wallet. His face looked strained, cheek blotchy, as if he'd blown up a stubborn beach ball. He scribbled on a napkin, and Anna folded the white square into a smaller square. Looking at the man, she slipped the wad of tissue under the band encircling her hat. Now the man gripped her wrist and he moved her hand back and forth. The room filled with strained voices. Buddy walked with the cramped gait of somebody who sat at a desk for twelve hours a day. He made the end of the table as the man shot the red weight down the board. It speeded down the table to where the blue weight hung on the edge. Thwack! Down went the blue weight; skidding, the red one took its spot. There were groans.

"You bumped off my one shot," Millie said. Their drinks sat half-full and looked warm.

At that moment, Anna slinked by and vanished in the crowd. A few seconds later, the man followed, puffy-cheeked, his hands in his pockets and whistling, like somebody trying to look inconspicuous.

"Where are the girls?" Logan asked when Buddy reached the table.

"Anna went outside," Buddy said. "I told you."

"Haven't you understood? Let her have her scheme. She likes to complicate everything, loves the drama." He nudged Buddy's elbow. "You have to stop doing what you think they want you to do. Do the opposite. Let them come to you."

It was a dry spell, Buddy thought. Nothing lasted forever. He planned to make a date with the girl on the day shift with a Greek fishing cap; what was her name? It started with an E. Effie? Epinephrine? No. Splurge on payday. Go to the bar in the hotel on Nob Hill. Gaze at the city lit like Las Vegas on the night of the world heavyweight title bout. In this corner, weighing in at a hundred and seventy pounds, Buddy Gosh!

Logan was waving his hand. He snapped his fingers. "I'm hungry. Are you hungry?"

Buddy blinked. "I could eat something."

"I feel like a hot dog. You? Wanna do a dog? What the hell time is it anyway?"

Lurching in the chair, Logan grabbed Buddy's hand and turned it over so he could see Buddy's wrist.

"Official Greenwich Mean Time is late as fuck. Give me a minute, we're skipping out."

Logan stood unsteadily, he wobbled then regained his footing, and he walked in a pattern to the phone. Glancing at the yellow sheet of paper in his hand, he closed the door of the phone booth. Buddy was hungry. The supermarket was open twenty-four hours and they could buy a tub of potato salad, bratwurst, sauerkraut, rolls, and cook the sausages at his apartment to stave off tomorrow's hangover, which was coming early. It was already here. Buddy dreaded how he would feel later today. It was going to be gross.

Buddy went outside for some fresh air while Logan made his phone call. A fight was breaking up and

Buddy saw Anna slumped on the curb, sobbing, a strap from her dress slipping down. Somebody lay on the ground and a young guy was kicking at the person, whoever he was. Anna's nose dripped blood and she held her ribcage. Nobody paid her any mind. The guy doing the kicking looked worn-out, liable to trip over himself. He had a whole gang with him, and they were laughing and pointing: they looked like kids. Anna got to her feet, strode into the middle of the group, and knelt by the person on the ground, whom Buddy recognized as the man from the shuffleboard table.

"Are you all right," she asked the man, "do you want me to call an ambulance?"

The shuffleboard player struggled up and then broke into a saggy jog. Anna was edging back when a boy of about sixteen walked up to her and yanked the tail of his flannel shirt to one side. Buddy had to do something. When he hiccupped, he somehow chanced upon a memory tucked away for a long time, a school fight with a bully that he ended with a few clumsy punches and halfhearted grabbing and shoving. Peeling away a layer of fear, Buddy pictured himself as a bull getting ready to charge a matador. Tentatively at first and then with gathering force, he burst forward; gaining momentum he body-slammed the kid. Buddy watched the kid's eyes roll back into his head.

They were shouting; he was hiccupping. His glasses sat askew on his nose. The kid scrambled to his feet, cocked his arm and punched wildly, hitting Anna in the jaw, and she crumpled, went down, and the guy started kicking her in the leg. Her hat rolled down the street. The kid yanked her around by the hair. Buddy gave himself a pep-talk. They are afraid. Go for them individually. Aim for their eyes. He slapped, jabbed, and gouged. The whole time he kept swinging, and when he swung, his fist smacked slippery flesh. Because they were short, his relative height let him rain down blows on them. He never aimed low but struck their faces, knuckles against their cheeks. A nose snapped. He heard loose jowly thuds. He caught one guy with his mouth gaping and heard the jawbone crack like a desiccated twig. They tried to flank him. He swung roundhouses, threw upper cuts; he blocked them like a lineman; at one point, he stepped on a guy's head, smashing his mouth on the pavement.

By now, the lights were shining along the block. Buddy became aware of sirens; his glasses lay on the far-away looking pavement. Then he was standing in the street, speckled with spattered drops of blood, stuffing the glasses in his breast pocket. Anna was sobbing, sniffling, and then keening a mournful wail. While the kids sat dazed on the curb, drooping chins, Anna tugged on Buddy's belt and he let her lead him. As they walked, she listed into him, and he veered away, but they kept bumping into each other. Finally, she wrapped her arm around his waist.

"I don't want people to fight," she said. "I hate this kind of violence."

His fingers raked her disheveled hair, caught in the tangled ends.

"Where's your hat?"

"Somewhere back there, I don't care about it now."

"It was brave to help the man, were you scared?"

"No, were you?"

"I wasn't thinking, I guess I'm scared now." Buddy felt surprisingly sober all of a sudden. He went on, exploiting this brief interlude of clear-thinking. "Next time if you need to call help," he said, "don't make an announcement about doing it."

They were walking under the light of the moon. A traffic light bobbed on a cable. The yellow lamp clicked on then off.

"Can you see?" she said. "Your clothes are stained. You must bleach the shirt."

"It's okay, that's what drycleaners are for."

"And you left the suits Logan gave you in the bar."

He started to turn. "I can go back."

She grabbed his belt. "The police will be arriving there soon."

"Me, I don't care. I'm not exactly an impressive physical specimen. Do you think they will arrest me?"

"They will want a statement," Anna said earnestly.

"They can come find me."

"It won't be hard, they can find anybody. What will you say about leaving the scene?"

"I saw the man on the ground, I saw you. Everything else dissolved; my mind locked itself. I guess I threw down, as they say. Self-defense."

Buddy saw himself swinging his arms, saw the kids try to flank him, and he didn't let them but kept punching. He was shocked at the idea he'd stepped on a guy's head.

They were walking under the overpass when a taxi stopped by the off-ramp. Anna's hat poked out. Buddy watched Anna shrug and then she broke into a quick-footed shuffle. There were no words. The wide-brimmed hat made a floppy halo as she tugged at the ends of the cord.

The roof light revealed Logan and Millie. At the window, Anna leaned down. They talked for several minutes. Buddy approached at intervals. He could hear them clearly now.

"Say it," Logan said. "Tell me."

"I am your—," Anna said.

"What?"

"You know," she said, bashfully.

"But I want to hear you say it loud and clear before you get in this cab."

"I. Am. Your. Lover!"

The door swung open and Anna scooted inside and became a shadow. The brim of the hat appeared in the window, white elbow, forearm, a hand unclenching. Tiny pieces of paper drifted like a puff of dandelion seeds. The arm was retracted. The hat swiveled. Buddy watched as the taxi glided away in the colorless morning. Buddy had finally faced the truth. Nobody ever looked back.

WE NEVER HAPPENED

There. It happened. In her head, Rachael was like, what? No way. It was incredible. Would anybody believe her if she told them what happened? She barely trusts her own memory: a bended-knee proposal, wedding, lawful marriage. They lasted for three days. He wedded her, bedded her, and dumped her. Literally, three days of marital bliss! A story on the front page of a tabloid: "Newlywed Calls it Quits on Honeymoon" or "Groom Jilts Bride Three Days After Wedding." Of course, she had doubts about their marriage. Maybe they'd break up. Maybe he'd get cold feet. Maybe one day they'd get divorced. Half of all marriages ended anyway, infidelity, irreconcilable differences, this thing, that thing, whatever, but three days? Oh, Lester, why?

Calm down, Rachael tells her herself. What you feel is emotional shock. Relax, focus. She glances at the counter. Coffee dribbles down the carafe and a drop hisses on the burner. In the bell-shaped crock, the butter's surface is strewn with spheres of water as if somebody has cried there. Rachael clenches her jaw, her ears begin buzzing from the pressure. This is all a bad dream. I'll wake up and we'll put everything back together. We'll view that bungalow in the avenues we always dreamed of and talk about wallpapering the spare bedroom for a kid.

Rachael sits side-saddle on the couch, as the pieces continue to fall. There is somebody else. Lester has met another woman. This woman modeled for the life-drawing classes. They bumped into each other in the hall, she was rushing about in a dressing gown. The woman recognized Lester's name from the gallery in the arts annex. Some photographers documented subjects, she told him, but his images interpreted them. They made statements. They said something. They discussed his handiwork, and who he was as an artist. I see you, the woman told Lester, in your photographs: a deserted back alley, a ramshackle stairwell of a clapboard building, a faceless robed statue atop the parapet of a skyscraper, a bulletin board covered in tattered fliers. You're wounded, she said: I'm wounded too. We're both wounded.

That was laying it on pretty thick, Rachael thinks.

"I don't know how I feel," Lester says as he paces the hall in their shared apartment. "I thought I could deal with it. I thought it would go away."

Rachael's whole frame trembles and her mind crackles with emotion. Choking up, Lester speaks as though saddened that life had fooled them both. He never planned to hurt anybody. He was lonely. He didn't know what to do; he likes being with her. It was out of his hands. It was all some kind of mistake. What could he do? Think about how he felt. It had nothing to do with any shortcomings on Rachael's part.

"I could've have kept everything to myself. At least I'm telling you," Lester says, absolving himself of guilt.

The inside of her mouth dries up and her throat constricts. Thoughts move through her mind. So Lester loved this somebody else? He never touched her, never kissed her. The skin on Rachael's forehead crinkles. Oh, this is bad. Rachael had hoped for a chance. She understood. Things happened. We can't control everything. But if he loved her, then poof! Their relationship is gone. Well, not gone, but over.

"What about me?" Rachael asks him.

"You're a good woman. You deserve better."

Rachael pouts at his response, sticking out her lower lip. Her nose leaks and she sneezes twice, putting her hand over her nose and mouth.

"Everybody is sick, now I'm getting sick." Her voice croaks like a frog tipsy on helium. She clutches a wad of shredded tissue, then changes her mind about why she's sneezing. "No, I'm not sick. This is an allergy."

"I have to go to the restroom," Lester says. He doesn't close the bathroom door all the way and she can see him standing by the toilet. Something reckless comes over her, a thought tickles her mind and she steps inside the bathroom. She walks over to him and with a forsaken expression on her face, she brushes his curly hair and strokes his face. Her fingernails are painted with a flesh-colored nail polish and caress his freckled nose, the skin taut over the bridge.

"This is me," she says. "I'm real. I'm here."

He scoops her up so that her knees wedge inside the crook of his elbows. He breathes heavily as he carries her over the threshold of the bedroom and drops her on the mattress. Legs spraddled, she watches him twist his head away and mash his face in the pillow. He never opens his mouth. It is happening. It is not purely physical. He is doing what she wants. Muscles straining, like a sailor staggering ashore from a shipwreck, he clings tight to her. He makes her flesh gasp. She wonders why do people crave the wrong things? Of course, she'd read stories by Edgar Allan Poe. These impulses are perverse: the urge to do the thing that will hurt you. He winds things up quickly, and a finger burrows in the small of her back. A startled cry breaks from her throat. Her body floats, her limbs tingle, the mattress hurls up, bump-jolt-whoosh, like when a jet lands and everything shudders and squeaks. There. It happens. It keeps happening.

They lie sprawled and naked on the full-sized mattress for a while. She stares at him and the cold begins to seep in, a patch of goosebumps dimple her abdomen. She wants to put on her leggings, zip her skirt and crawl inside her sweater, but he holds her still. He traces the appendix scar on her stomach: wide as a finger, wrinkled like a flattened earthworm, it creases the side of her lap. He yawns, shivers. Then he wipes his palm on her abdomen. Rachael forces a smile and tries to coax her brain to feel happiness. Of course, they still had sex. She did sleep with him. But when he begins prying himself loose, something also unclenches inside her, loosening its grip, and slips away.

"It's us," she says firmly. "This is us."

"What?" Lester says. Glowering, he plucks a tissue from the box. "That's not me, that's you."

That afternoon Rachael begins packing her things. Shoeboxes totter in stacks of twos and threes. A hard-shell suitcase lies splayed open on the floor. The room has become a den filled with cardboard boxes, piled up to her waist. The boxes lean against the wall and block the door. Yellow strips of masking tape dangle limply from the moving boxes. Rachael repeatedly tapes down the disobedient tape, which tangles as she frantically starts taping the boxes up again. While unrolling a strip of tape, she remembers something from her childhood. She sees herself as a toddler, wailing inconsolably, as her family taped boxes for a move. They always moved. She never stopped hating the noise of taping up boxes: it is the sound of leaving.

Her mother is stacking clothes for the move: blouses, slacks, slips, panties, leggings, tights. Her mother is a buxom woman, front-heavy, she walks leaning backwards to offset the imbalance of her paunchy stomach and sagging breasts. The skin beneath her nose is always red and her lips are perpetually chapped.

"Talk to me," Rachael's mother says, "I can be your sounding-board."

"I don't know what to do. Should we stay?"

"I think he's waiting for us to get out. He wouldn't want to run into me right now."

"I keep hoping, maybe, for something."

"You've stayed here enough, you did your best."

"I paid half the deposit, half the rent, and the

month's just beginning." Rachael looks down.

"We can put you up for as long as you need."

"I guess we can take what we can carry then," Rachael says, realizing that this is really happening, this is her life now.

After all the boxes are loaded in the trunk of her mother's Camry, Rachael scribbles her parents' phone number on a slip of paper and leaves it on Lester's kitchen table. She paces the hallway, looking at Lester's collection of hats on the coat-tree: the crushable fedora, the straw panama, the beanie, the Cossack kepi. Why did you do this to me? She feels she is talking silently to Lester's spirit. I never needed anybody until I met you. I cooked for you and cleaned for you, took care of you. I was someone you could talk to about your day, your work. She deliberately leaves the door to the apartment unlocked when she steps out into the hallway, for the last time. All of Lester's hats, the music system, stacks of records, the shoebox full of baseball cards and concert ticket stubs inside.

In the sedan, her mother tries to cheer Rachael up by talking about completely unrelated things. Please hold on, she says: sudden stops are sometimes necessary. Do they still have the sign on the buses? Rachael nods: I think so. Her mother is riding the brake pedal. This is how I drive, she says, keeping the needle below the speed limit. They stop at a red light. Rachael stares at her mother, wondering does she think she is driving an eighteen-wheeler? People look at them. Their car screeches away, takes the corner like they're driving in the Daytona 500. Rachael grips the armrest but it doesn't help. When the car lurches, she feels herself thrown from the seat. Her mother's face crinkles in bafflement; she is sitting about ten inches from the steering wheel.

"Why do you keep losing your footing?"

Rachael shoots back. "Do you want me to drive?"

"You have to hold on tight!"

They drive together in silence. It begins to drizzle and Rachael's eyes roll back, her lids flutter, she sags down in her seat, relaxing. Her memory falters. She feels out of sync, like she'd been thrown out of the space-time continuum. Today already seems long past and she can't remember what she did a second ago. How did this happen, how did I get here? She feels like she needs to get somewhere, to be doing something, but she has lots of time to get to wherever she is going. Everything is rushing past and Rachael wants to mash the brakes. Outside, a pile of bald tires lie on the sidewalk, nearing the end of the line. Then Rachael falls asleep, goes dreamy, and when she awakens, it's dark out.

"You must be exhausted from the strain."

"Oh, my, how long was I out for?" Rachael asks her mother.

"A few minutes, you hunched over, started snoring. I thought you were joking."

"I was dreaming. I forget what about."

"I'm concerned. Your forehead is sweaty."

"What? It's okay." Rachael wipes her forehead. "Low blood sugar, I think. I missed lunch." She is staring at the fold of skin under her mother's chin. "Wait. Did I eat anything?"

Steering in silence, her mother leans over the

console and pulls some chocolate from her handbag. Rachael breaks off a piece and tentatively bites down on it before consuming the candy bar. She crumples the candy wrapper into a wad.

This is no dream, it's really happening.

Rachael and her mother park along the curb outside the house. Her mother switches off the engine. Rachael unlatches the seatbelt and gets out of the car. Looking at the house, she thinks nothing is different, nothing has changed. But she barely recognizes the rest of the block. There are pastel split-level houses with concrete walkways; each home has a bay window, with drawn fringed curtains. We have nothing to hide, they say. To her left old eucalyptus trees straggle in the median, placed there to soften the noise of traffic. But Rachael feels the trees are really saying: this space belongs to us, to nature.

"I know things seem bad," her mother says, "we can call our lawyer."

Rachael is barely listening. She watches a bus pull away from the shelter, a passenger tripping backwards.

Rachael's mother continues saying whatever pops into her head. "You look all alone in your own little world. Would it hurt so much to smile? Let me see you smile. Can you?"

Rachael clenches her teeth. When she was younger, she had the inkling that nobody liked her mother. Cringing at a table in a restaurant, she'd side with the waitress, I know how she makes you feel, and I'm sorry for her behavior: I'm nothing like her.

Rachael's mother makes sounds like a duck quacking.

"You're crying?" Rachael asks her mother, out of shock. Then, indignantly: "why are you crying?"

"This isn't crying," her mother says. "I'm just choked up, it's hormonal."

Rachael never saw her mother cry for any reason before. Rachael watches the drop trickle down her mother's face. Her mother gives Rachael a look that makes her feel like she's a small child being chastised.

"I don't know what to do," her mother says. "I feel responsible." She dabs a wet cheek. "I should've kept my mouth shut, did I push you?"

"I'm going to be all right one day."

"What do I know? I hate that you're hurting. I wish I could take this pain from you."

"I know. Somehow things are going to work out. It's going to be okay, Mom, I think."

"I still can't believe it. How could he? I can't understand it. It's as if he married you so that he could break up with you."

"I thought the same thing all day. It's bad. It's the worst thing that could happen. Now I know what bad feels like."

"Your father and I had our hiccups. We fought, he drank. This is worse than anything."

"When things get better, I'll be grateful for small blessings. I know the worst now."

"I hope so. We only want what's best for you. We want you to have it all."

When Rachael turned thirty, her mother told her that she'd reached a difficult age for women to meet people, male or female, and make new friends, let alone develop a long-term relationship. Rachael's biological clock must be ticking, her mother intimated. If Rachael wanted to have children, she needed to begin right away. After thirty, the odds get longer, and soon all bets are off. Her mother confided that her own parents had had her late, and she was practically an only child because her other siblings were so much older. They never had time for me, she said, then whispering: I think I was an accident. She believed that her parents resented her and they never advised her about anything. She made mistakes. So she made a vow to herself to do things differently with Rachael. She poured everything she had into Rachael. She wanted to give to her daughter what she never had.

But growing up, Rachael became rebellious. No matter what she didn't want to end up like her mom. Over her dresser, she hung a mirror that read "this is what a feminist looks like," and she hatched a plan to trace her family's history to find the oldest last name on the female side and to legally change her last name to what she found. Rachael stayed out late; she drank, had sex with whomever. She did everything. She never told anybody. It meant nothing. She didn't have to explain anything. Things just happened. At one point, when her lovelife stalled, she ran several personal ads in the paper. She needed to kick-start that lovelife. She sought a dangerous poet, handy with a wrench; a few vices were permissible. She fantasized about having eggs broken over her body in a bath tub. She'd call the recording service and the voice would tell her she had fifty messages. Every day, a small stack of letters, with photographs, arrived in the mail. The men asked her what she liked to do. They told her what they liked to do, and how they liked it done. She let a man take off her shirt and then made out with him on the floor, tongues tussling, on a section of carpet. He fucked her halfheartedly and afterwards they smoked a joint as they lay tangled clumsily together on the floor. They listened to Frank Zappa and laughed.

But one day Rachael woke up on another floor, a mosquito hummed in her ear, and a girl's face peered down at her. The girl had a wispy mustache and melancholy hazel eyes. She was sucking a menthol lozenge, clicking it against her teeth. The girl wore a hotel maid's uniform. Get yourself cleaned up, the girl said, you smell like kitty litter. When Rachael sat up her neck ached almost as if she had whiplash. Can you help me stand? Rachael asked the maid. I need to use the toilet. She glanced about the deserted bathroom and saw herself in the mirror, she looked awful. Was she trying to get herself roughed up? Rachael was lucky nobody dragged her out in the street. No more close calls. She felt relieved, fortunate that no bones were broken, no missing teeth.

When Rachael met Lester she doubted anything would happen. She never saw herself settling down. But slowly she liked him and one day she thought: I love him. She had never fallen in love. Sometimes she mistreated him. When he came on too strong, she acted aloof. She disliked doing it. But she thought she needed proof he wanted her. Finally, she believed: I have a boyfriend. They never planned anything. They talked about how nobody got married anymore. Nobody had kids. All of a sudden, and on bended knee, he proposed.

I'll marry you, he said. We'll be tradition's rebels. We can be man and wife; or husband and wife; we can have a whole brood of kids, as many as you want, and we can watch them grow up, and they can visit us when we get old. Rachael thought he was joking. No. He meant it. He wanted to do it right away, as soon as she was ready. So it happened. And here she was.

Tonight Rachael drifts in and out of sleep, dreaming she went to a clinic with him. While they sat in the waiting room, she disrobed, peeling off each article of clothing, and began anointing her body with a lotion. She had some kind of sickness. When the nurse called her name, Lester ushered her down a flight of stairs, poised to sweep her into his arms if she should stumble. At the bottom, Lester spread a cloak over a puddle of water in front of the doctor's office. Then the results came in. It was good news, everybody cried. There was only one thing. She needed to extract a molar. The doctor placed a pair of tweezers in her hand and Rachael opened her mouth wide and put her hand inside and wiggled the tooth back and forth until she managed to drag the tooth out of her gums.

In the morning Rachael sits cross-legged on the floor of her childhood bedroom, flipping through albums in a fruit crate. She plays the fussy waddling violin intro of "Street Hassle" over and over. The melody plays in her head after she lifts the needle. As she mouths the lyrics, quavering and shaky, her throat clots and her eyes tingle. She uses the bathroom, scours the toilet bowl, and sprays the sink with foaming cleanser. She swings open the medicine cabinet: dad's things, mom's things. She unfolds the wax-coated wrapper from a two-sided razor and stares at the blade in her palm. Then she dashes to the bedroom and in the dark squats down on her haunches, whimpering, while she slaps herself in the face.

"Are you hurt?" It is her father speaking.

"I'll be okay," she says. "Don't come in."

"Take as long as you need."

She hears him waiting for her to say something else. "Thank you. I might."

When Rachael leaves her room she looks like a person walking barefoot over gravel. In the kitchen, her mother is preparing a late breakfast and has begun by mutilating a bell pepper, poking in the stem and scraping out the seeds. Then she puts the pieces into melted butter, along with two eggs, and mixes them all together with a whisk.

"You should sit," her father says, "you look very tired, really tired."

Her father is reading the newspaper. He is balding and combs a strand of hair back with his fingers. Rachael sits at the table and her mother sets down the plate and pours coffee into a mug with a chipped brim.

"I can't understand people anymore," her father says. "Nothing makes sense." His shaggy eyebrows bristle and squirm, squashed caterpillars. "You have to wonder." He pours cornflakes into a bowl.

Rachael looks at her father. He is a sturdy, built man who sets the alarm for oh-dark-thirty, as he likes to say, and then walks five miles on the treadmill in the den. As a child, she awoke to clunking barbells and thudding ankle-weighted feet. Her father drank to excess and smoked heavily too. I have an addictive temperament, he used to say. But one day he poured all the whiskey down the drain. And he threw the pack of cigarettes in a trash can in the street. He started running marathons. Each day is a blessing, he says now. Don't count the days; make the days count.

"I was at the bowling alley," her father tells them. "I see this fat fellow with blubbery arms, shoulders shrugging continuously. He gasped like a pregnant woman nine months gone on a hot humid day. He poked these plump fingers into a size-eight. I actually cringed." Her father stops to eat some cereal before he continues his story. "Then he hoists the ball and I peek at the back of his head, and he has the number eight tattooed sideways on his neck. And I'm thinking: why not make the eight stand upright? I don't know why people mess with symbols."

The old man's eyes brighten as he continues to talk about his bowling adventure.

"But he was a natural phenomenon. Unwieldy bulk or no, nothing stops him, and this man crouches, swings back his arm, and lumbers ahead, kind of stop-action, herky-jerky. The way he moved, I thought he'd wrench his back. Then he tosses the ball down the lane, I never saw one spin so fast. Like in a movie, the lane receded into space, going on forever, and this man with this weird eight tattoo stands there observing the ball's progress, and I keep waiting for the crash of the pins, but it's taking a long time, and this thought pops into my head: nothing lasts forever. I felt peace, and I thought, thank goodness."

Her mother asks. "How many did he get?"

The old man's face scowls. "Huh?"

"How many pins did the man knock down, did he get a strike?"

"Oh, that's not the point. Anyway, I forget. But everybody cheered. Something big must've happened."

This evening the phone rings and Rachael picks up the receiver, but the person on the other end doesn't say anything so she hangs up the phone. After she cradles the handset, the phone rings again.

"I know you hate me right now," Lester says. "I need to explain."

She waits for ten seconds in silence.

"In case you're wondering, I'm not seeing her."

Rachael hangs up. The phone rings again. When the message machine beeps, his voice says, "Come on, Rachael, I know you're there."

She lifts the receiver out of the cradle.

"I never touched her. Once I could have her, I didn't want her anymore. It was something I needed to get out of my system. It was never real. I was afraid."

"What do you want?"

"I don't know what makes me do it. I'm getting help. It's awfully expensive. I see a psychotherapist once a week."

Rachael holds her breath then exhales. "Look, I have to go."

"All I ask is you give me another chance. I'm trying to become a better person."

"Please don't call me again. I'm talking to a lawyer. I might sue you for mental cruelty and psychological suffering. I'm serious."

"It can't end this way," he says. "I was hoping. Maybe we have a chance to start again, patch things up. If it's meant to be, that is. If not, I want us to part as friends. We were together for four years. You were my first serious girlfriend."

Rachael eases the handset into the cradle and watches the phone. She stomps to the kitchen, uncorks the wine and gulps a mouthful. In the window pane, her reflection wiggles its head.

Today Rachael is thinking about how a dilemma begins. I knew I was late. The signs are clear. Even before she knew, she knew. Bloating, nausea, breasts like gourds, a hung-over queasiness, disgust at fragrances and perfumed bathroom sprays. She feels this reckless joy for no reason. But she's alive. She no longer mourns. She loves everybody and every second matters. She pukes, vomits, throws up, heaves. Her memory is foggy. The clinic runs a blood test, and she holds the dot-matrix printout. Result: Positive. Seated in the scuffed-wax corridor, she keeps mouthing the words, result-positive. She is going to have a baby. How many weeks? It must be eight weeks. That's how long it's been since the last time she and Lester had sex. She never expected this. They had taken every precaution but somehow this miracle happened and now she's pregnant. She wants to yell, I'm expecting!

Her father looks at her quizzically, waiting for something. "Expecting what?"

"Oh," her mother says. "I'm going to be a granny." She twists in the chair. Outside in the street, a garbage truck heaves and jerks rambunctiously. Suddenly, her mother's face twitches, pinches. She looks as though the sun is blinding her. "Who—?" She freezes then thaws. "Is there any question? Is it his?"

Rachael nods. "I need to talk to him."

"I wonder. He might think you want to trap him."

"We always talked about kids. He likes kids. He told me he thought marriage was an outdated concept unless you wanted to have kids. Kids were the only reason for getting married."

Her mother draws a breath, lowers her chin, and exhales through her nose.

"Do you know where he lives now? It seems he fell off the face of the earth."

"I doubt he ever moved. He always was a homebody. I bet he's hunkered down in the flat with his hats and records and the baseball cards, wondering how he screwed up so much."

"You need to be strong. I know you can be. You're scrappy, a tough cookie. But I'll hate it if you get your hopes up only to get hurt again."

"I'll be fine. I feel like a mongoose." She claws the air, bares her teeth, makes hissing noises.

They meet this morning at a diner near the ocean. Smells waft of bacon frying and scorched coffee. They are seated in bentwood chairs, at a table with uneven legs, and she orders poached eggs, rye toast and sausage links. She pokes at the food, sips the coffee. The eggs taste warm and rubbery, like unsweetened marshmallows; the yolks are deep yellow. He is buttering a plain bagel, elbows planted to keep the table from tipping.

"I don't know how it happened," she says. "Well, I guess it was that day."

"You're sure?"

As he peels open the jelly container, she tells him about the blood test. "Result: positive."

"I mean, it's mine, right?"

"I was so happy, but I knew you'd take it the wrong way, but then I couldn't keep it to myself any longer so I told you."

He loads a blob of scrambled egg on the bagel and chomps down. "I can go with you," he says, mouth full, "if you want to not have it."

She watches him gulp a slug of coffee and swallow.

"I thought about that," she says. "I turn thirty-five this year. I don't have forever."

Nobody says anything for a minute. When he takes a bite of the bagel, his elbow comes up and the table lists. He grabs the edges and wrestles with the table, inching the pedestal for a firm purchase on the floorboards. Finally, he kneels.

"I never thought of myself as a father," he says. He folds a napkin and wedges it under the base. "I'm not the type. Some guys do a good job. They change the diaper, cradle the kid, make kooky noises, tickle them, chuckling tee-hee, when the kid nurses their shirt or spews formula on their pants. But me, if there's a father gene, I don't have it."

She swallows now. "Why did we even get married then? I thought you wanted kids."

His eyes squeeze shut and he shakes his head. He drops into the bentwood and stares at his shoe for so long she glances down to see what he is looking at but there is nothing except his shoe: a black shiny oxford.

"I'm sorry," he says after a few seconds. "I'm taken aback. It's a shocker."

"What about me? You want me back then you push me away." She shakes her head, her brain at an impasse.

His hand curls over hers. "Do you still love me?"

"I know I used to, I really did."

He draws back his hand. "So you don't anymore?"

"Maybe I do. I could again."

Eyes blinking, she wonders how she might respond if he tries to kiss her.

"Tell me how to help," he says. "Whatever you want me to do, I'll do it."

"I want you to go with me to the doctor."

The next minute lasts forever. An hour seems to pass. Seconds slip by.

"All right," he says, eyes flickering. "I can come. You know, I want to, I really do."

"Thank you." Something tugs inside her stomach and she wants to hug him.

"No need," he says. His jaw clenches then relaxes. "I'd regret not coming."

The waiting room resembles a den or parlor or private library with easy chairs and an array of floor lamps, each with a glass shade like an upside-down cake-bell. After answering the questions on the form, she sits and waits for her turn. A nurse in green scrubs calls Rachael's name. Lester offers his hand and pulls her to her feet.

In the examination room, she unbuckles her belt

and raises her blouse. A patch of goosebumps rises on her tummy. The nurse lays her hands on the little mound.

"Already puffy," she says. "You're showing early."

"I'm just out of shape. I always had belly fat."

"I can wait outside," Lester says.

"I'm not uncomfortable."

Then the doctor comes into the room. She wears beige corduroys, white lab coat, blond hair pulled back on the sides. Her creased face glances at Rachael's abdominal scar, and the doctor furrows her brow.

"That's quite a scar," the doctor says. "I hardly see scars like that now. We barely make a wrinkle."

"There were complications," Rachael says as the nurse inflates the blood pressure cuff on Rachael's arm, and she glances at Lester. "I remember the pain and the bloating like it happened yesterday."

It happened when she was seventeen. She'd felt sick all day so she drank several cans of beer, which didn't help. She lay in her bed clutching the pillow against her abdomen, shivering from the pain. Finally she went to the hospital. Every day she was in the hospital the nurse switched her IV-bag, and the doctor came in and raised the blanket. A tube had been inserted in the incision for drainage. They kept her for eight days.

"My appendix had become gangrenous and tangled, and it burst during the surgery. I was lucky. It could've been worse."

"You might've died," Lester says.

The doctor nods then moves around the stethoscope, licking her lips. "There's your heartbeat, we got yours, loud and clear." She puckers her lips.

"What?"

"Nothing," she says, glancing away. She keeps moving the stethoscope. "Let's try something else."

Rachael melts in the chair, while Lester grips her hand, beaming at her. My husband, she thinks, is it okay to call him that? The doctor moves the gadget back and forth over Rachael's stomach, looking more concerned. Lester's smile is slipping. The doctor stands up, and sighs, still staring at the screen. "I'm sorry," the doctor says.

"What do you mean?" Lester asks.

The doctor ignores him; she is standing up.

"You're at ten weeks; and there's no heartbeat."

Lester's face scrunches up. "How can you be sure?"

"The heart beating flickers and pulsates like a little light bulb."

The doctor walks out; Rachael is alone with Lester again, and is zipping up her pants.

"I don't understand," she says. Her head throbs. She closes her eyes. Am I here? Did this just happen? Biting her lip, she begins to grieve, trying not to show any emotion. I never guessed this would happen. As Rachael walks through the waiting room, the pregnant women glance up. Why did she tell anyone she was pregnant? Now people will ask about the due date, and she'll lower her head, mutter something inane, some platitude, because the truth is there is no more due date. There is only today; how will she ever get past today?

It is November and cold rain falls. It is a long walk to the garage. When they get inside Lester's car, Lester breaks down. They spend several minutes crying, grabbing each other. This is a sorrow that has waited for some time. But she feels no better for letting it out.

Looking out the windshield, Lester sniffles. "It was a journey I'm glad I took with you." He is trembling. "Thank you."

"We should get a second opinion," he continues. "The doctor barely looked at you. Maybe it's too early. They make mistakes all the time."

Pain stabs the creases in her lap at the edges of her crotch. Blood, she feels a trickling, as if something unlocked and tumbled out of her. "There's no baby anymore," Rachael says. "It's dead."

This doctor looks young in the face, barely thirty, with smooth cheeks, but his hair, though thick, is turning gray at the temples. He is chewing gum intermittently. He prints out a copy of the ultrasound. Looking at the image, he says, "yeah." The print-out shows a black pouch, empty except for a tiny speck at the bottom, surrounded by staticky snow. The doctor lets it sink in; his body language tells her to take her time. Rachael is beginning to come round.

"Was it because I drank?"

"How much do you drink?"

"I had some wine."

"I doubt a glass or two makes much difference. Do you smoke?"

She shakes her head. On the wall, a slew of photographs, some in black and white, some in color, show him shaking hands each time with a different woman who is lying in a different hospital bed, holding a different baby in her arms. The doctor's hair is thick and dark in the pictures. This work has aged him.

"Nothing I say is going to make you feel better. People want to blame themselves." He twists his fingers. "But it could be a chromosomal mismatch, and the pregnancy basically shut itself down."

How many times per week does he have this conversation? Rachael wonders. At least they got the news early. She'd barely got used to the idea: maternity. Think about somebody finding out at eight months. The grief would cripple you. Or multiple times, serial miscarriages. They can tell you that it's a mercy, a blessing in disguise, and that you'll bounce back. In a year or two, you'll have a baby, if you want one, or more. You can have a whole bunch if you want, the doctor says, echoing Lester's words. But you have to have faith. You have to believe. Her time would come.

But right now, he tells Rachael, they have to figure out something.

"Get this taken care of. Don't wait. Removal will accelerate the healing process. The procedure is straightforward. If everything goes as planned, you'll be on your way in a few hours."

"Will you do it, or is there somebody else?"

He nods and pats his heart. "I will."

"I'm sorry," Rachael says, genuinely apologetic. "I didn't mean anything by it. You seem so young."

"I get the comment a lot. But I'm older than I appear. It's called being undercover old."

The doctor chats with her. For some reason, he tells her that he never planned to become a doctor. In college, he studied philosophy and literature, and he wanted to write. Then he learned that Chekhov trained in medicine. And this young man, Rachael's doctor, tells her he speculated that Chekhov's background must have prepared him to diagnose the society and times in which he lived. Her doctor says he learned of many author-doctors and doctor-poets and he enrolled in courses in biology and chemistry and took the MCAT and was happy to learn he was accepted to the UCSF School of Medicine.

"I wanted to help people, especially women."

Suddenly, Rachael hugs the doctor. She burrows her face into his shoulder, wipes her nose on his white coat. She needs to breathe and she turns her head from side to side. He begins to wrest himself free. After a few seconds, the muscles in her arms relax, and he scoots his chair away. She schedules for late in the day on Friday, giving her the whole weekend to recover. She lies in a hospital bed in a cubicle with an expanse of pale curtain drawn across for privacy. Lester reads poems to her: Hardy, Marvell, Hopkins, Eliot. "Macavity: the Mystery Cat" makes her laugh and it hurts, like coughing, but she has to laugh or she will cry. He reminisces about the time they compared song titles by Kate Bush and Iggy Pop: "Seek and Destroy" and "Room for a Life." She laughs silently and her belly tightens. Somebody yanks the protective curtain open.

"Hey, what's so funny?" A male nurse says. He sounds chipper. "What did I miss, talking about me again?" He cracks jokes about dancing. Then he stops smiling and becomes silent. He lays a yellow heart-shaped cushion on the bed and then withdraws and easefully closes the curtain. They wait for two hours.

Oh, why did she schedule this appointment so late in the day? Finally, the medical staff come for her.

"When this ordeal is done," Lester says, "I'll marry you again."

"We're already married."

"We have to figure something out."

"Maybe," she says, "we can stay together. I don't know. Let's see."

She feels sure he's heard her; he glances down at her and then saunters away.

Rachael is lying on the examination table, her feet hanging in stainless steel stirrups. She is unable to see anything down there. This is what it must seem like to stand naked and blindfolded in room full of onlookers. The doctor is looking inside her. I never wanted anybody to see inside me. But now they can see me. Her waist goes numb. The masked, bespectacled face at her ear tells her she should feel nothing, but she experiences a twinge, a scratch, a stabbing, then something scrapes the inside of her hip.

"I can feel something!" Like somebody dragging her bare across asphalt.

She is talking to herself. She says everything out loud, in a raspy voice, sometimes mere breaths of air, then yelling. Her body is quivering, her feet knocking in the stirrups. She shivers and yawns, but when the syringe empties into the IV bag, her bones melt and her whole body turns into a puddle of warmth.

While it is happening, her lids close halfway. She drifts. There are hallucinations. Projected in the back of her head she sees a puppy crate. A tiny waddle of white fur climbs the gate, a boy dog with a naked belly. He licks his front paw and dips his head. His back leg thumps; he is gnawing the binding of a textbook; he hunches his back, raises his nose and sniffs, then scampers away. On the floor lies a tiny sausage-colored mound.

(That was us. We *did* happen. Sort of.)

It is as if the best part of her life is over, and there's nothing to hold on to. Everything is slipping away.

It is the next day. It is a new day. Rachael stands in the shower, water pelts her skin like grains of scalding hail, the trace of chlorine stinging her eyes. Reluctantly, she washes her body. Squatting, she watches blood-streaked water gurgle in the drain. Her slippers snuffle and scrape on the floor. She straightens her back, adjusts the folds of the terrycloth bathrobe and cinches the drawstring. Then another day comes. Does the week start on Monday or Sunday? Is it still last week? Today is Sunday. Last week is over. It is the first day of the week. The new week is already here. It's beginning now.

The worst has happened. The grief is like being evicted and being escorted out of your home. The house where you lived is not your place anymore. Maybe nowhere is. She traces the marker's tip on the blank square on her calendar, a slash across yesterday. Now Thanksgiving is coming. She walks across the avenue to the mall and watches a movie about a late middle-aged husband who murders his longstanding mistress to preserve his marriage. Every day gets darker. The holiday season never ends. Sometimes she boards the metro, huddles in the one-person seat, and rides out all the way, sitting, staring, for fifteen minutes.

Snow falls but the flakes melt into the pavement. Each morning, she boils water for instant oatmeal, dresses, and goads herself into motion. Who she is has been dislocated, popped out of joint, and she is trying to snap herself back into place. Every day, she waits for the metro, clutching her handbag against her stomach. January outlasts every month so far. Thank goodness for work, thank goodness for chores and mindless tasks, and for fatigue and for sleep.

In February the sun shines meekly in the sky. It takes hours, but the sun burns off the morning mist. In the stores, the racks hold crimson heart-shaped boxes, pink greeting cards, and shiny silver balloons. Valentine's Day falls on Sunday, Monday is President's Day: a three-day weekend. They put the chocolates on sale. The racks have a picked-clean look. A man chooses a card from the empty bin. A woman herds a gang of children. They chatter and whoop, hands clutched to their chests, laughing, gleeful, at the windfall.

Will life always be like this?

Following dinner one night Rachael's mother opens an envelope and looks at the contents. She nods her head up an inch then down again, lips clenched. After a minute, she lays the sheets of the petition flat and nudges them across the table.

"We went back and forth with the lawyer."

"Does it really matter whether we get a nullity?"

Her mother sighs. "I think it's important. It was

fraudulence. Simple as that." She drums the table.

"We consummated the marriage."

"No. You were never married in the first place, because of the deception. That's what the lawyer says."

Rachael stares at the boxes on the petition. Her mother tucks her chin down.

"What deception," Rachael says, "what fraud?"

"Did he say he wanted children?"

"He said he did, I mean, kind of."

"But he told you later that he wanted no children?"

"I guess so."

"Then that's fraud, that's deception, and you need to sign your name here."

Holding the petition by the edge, she sets the pen on the line. Try not to think about penmanship. You always write so neatly, even your signature looks too careful, as if you're practicing cursive instead of signing your name. Come on, this is me. Sign the paper. For a moment, she sees herself with her mother, these two women clutching pens, then Rachael signs her name.

There. That was us too. We never happened.

BAD PENNY

Her name was Dalia Flinders. Her life ceased at age 39. She lay in a bed for days as doctors ran tests. He didn't know their names. They were looking for any signals of mental activity. But there was no miracle. They let her end. Doesn't everything always end? Your name is Boyd Sparks, he tells himself. You are 41 years old and you are retracing your steps, redoing that day, the day done that is never undone. Today Boyd mounts the same steps up Coit Tower that they climbed and he stands on the platform overlooking the bay. He's kept a list of places to revisit without Dalia. The wind comes off the ocean and a gust shoves him, slapping his cheek. Boyd staggers, plants his feet and braces himself. He remembers watching Dalia from this spot. Her peach hair sparkled in the sunlight. We were here, he tells himself. Flat rooftops clump down the hill; fog from the headlands floats over the bridge. What are you afraid of? It is the sky, seemingly whispering to him.

The wind forces his lips apart: I never thought I fell in love, I never thought I went crazy.

The words are whipped away by a gust.

He clutches the handrail and slowly treads down the steps, he is in no hurry. This day will end soon enough. The next item on his list is the machine in the lobby: the one under the painting of dozens of misshapen midget-workers. He remembers walking down the steps with Dalia, alert to catch her if she stumbled. Boyd thinks of Dalia, he is saying, "Wait," but she never looks back. A few more steps and Boyd reaches into his pocket and pulls out the penny he made that day in the penny souvenir machine: elongated, egg-shaped, imprinted with a miniature bridge. All the while he imagines Dalia stood there with him, talking. He sees her looking into the glass cube as he cranked the machine's handle, watching the wheels roll over the penny, then watching the coin be reincarnated into a new thing before their eyes. An elderly man passes by and he tips a sweat-crusted baseball cap at Boyd, then climbs up the steps in worn-down cowboy boots. After a moment, Boyd glances back up the stairs. Nobody is there. He can hear the old man's boots clop way up on the platform. Boyd hears himself, or at least this person he used to be, tell Dalia in fragments about what he planned so long to say.

"We've reached this stage," Boyd said that day. Her hand slipped, and she paused, mouth turned down at the corner. She listened quietly, skin turning amber-tinted under the light.

"I don't know what happened," she said, "the plans, looking at sheets, towels, dishes. The picnic set."

"I know," Boyd's former self said, his old self.

Boyd's new self watches Dalia's apparition take the penny from the tray.

"I knew something was coming," Dalia said that day. "Thanks a lot. For everything."

Eyes shut now, Boyd clenches the penny and shakes his head. "I should've told you," he says aloud. He is talking to the mural. But that day he stopped talking, glanced at her face, and then came out with "no matter what, I hope we can always stay friends." She walked away from him, stepping quietly, and thoughtfully made a circuit of the lobby.

"There's no point," she said. "We had everything, what else do you want?" Then she told him she wanted him to leave her alone. She lowered her chin. "I never wanted to be with you," she said. "But you made me want this."

Boyd remembers how she looked him squarely in the face, reading it, while emotions tugged at her own features. He wonders, didn't she know how he felt, couldn't she tell he'd cooled off? Once, long ago before that day when it all ended, he thought about her every hour, dreamed of her and woke up with her in his mind. Then the emotions flamed out and became manageable. Dalia receded from his mind and he seldom thought of her. But he kept postponing the talk they needed to have. But then that day the words just poured out of him.

"Time will tell," she said, "you'll be sorry. You'll wish you still had me. I won't be there. I'll be gone." Her eye seemed to melt and he watched as a drop sluiced the skin of her cheek. She blinked and wiped her face. He stared at a place over her head, mouth crinkled. "You're a fake," she said. "You're a liar. You're a—" She sighed. "Oh, just fuck you." She never swore, and then she stomped out of the building. Well, he told himself, how did you think she'd react? The truth was he never expected things to last long with her. Boyd sits in the front row of this memory. The volume is turned up all the way. Then the memory backs off as he rubs the flattened penny. Boyd can smell that late summer cool tucked in the branches of the evergreens and medicine smell of the eucalyptus trees.

Boyd met Dalia at work. The humming of his computer screen made him drowsy and lulled him to sleep. Then Dalia walked into the office one day. She barely spoke and they set up a makeshift desk in the back for her. Her job was to process advance orders for new versions of their company's software. A month after Dalia's arrival the staff gathered nervously in the kitchen area, grumbling about Mondays. Dalia sipped cola through a lipstick-smeared straw, and when she spoke, her voice sounded reluctant, tentative.

"My first meeting," she said.

"First waste of time is more like it," Boyd said. She giggled. Nobody knew her purpose there, but there were rumors. The gossip was that she was related to the company's owner through marriage. That she was average and lacked ambition. Someone said she had a kid but didn't know who the father was. Boyd also heard that she lived on her own in a studio-apartment in the avenues. Boyd had little reason to like her. Married once, he had no interest in anything long-term. Been down that route, he'd say. His marriage ended amicably: no children, no joint property, he and his wife had just grown apart. It was two years since he'd dated a woman: a twenty-something who wore yellow nail polish. He managed fine on his own. Nobody made claims; he belonged to himself. Dropped slacks on the floor. Draped a jacket over the chair. Cupboards left ajar, sink stacked with unwashed dishes. Sat with a book in his lap all afternoon, watched any old movie. But then one day he noticed that his and Dalia's paths crossed. It seemed she timed her break to overlap with his. She'd find him in the plaza, sitting under the madrona tree, and he'd brush off a spot and together they'd watch the teenagers play hacky-sack while they ate their food.

"You have good skin," Dalia said.

"I drink lots of water," Boyd said. He watched Dalia bite her sandwich. "Seeing anybody?" he asked.

At first, she nodded then swallowed her food and said "no, sorry, just kidding." So he asked her out and she said "why not?" Shortly thereafter they went out together for the first time.

In the morning after their date Dalia shook Boyd awake. "I was dreaming," she said, "what was I dreaming?" In the middle of the room, she put on his shirt and tried to do up the buttons, but the shirt was inside-out. Then Dalia sat on the edge of Boyd's twin mattress and described her dream. She saw herself hobbling along the street with a broken leg. A rope lowered down from the sky.

"Immediately I think, 'Oh great, I'm dead.' But it seemed like no big deal. Like somebody tagged me when I was kid or told me I had cooties." She snapped her fingers. "I was just like, darn it." Then she told Boyd that a man with a red meaty face and hairless arms rappelled down the rope face first. "Abseiling," she said. "That's what they call it."

She went on, becoming animated, acting out her dream. Grounded, the man from her dream put on a pair of horn-rimmed glasses. You know why I came? he asked, though his mouth never moved. She told Boyd she heard this question in her head, as if by telepathy. When Boyd asked her how she answered the man, Dalia said she just shrugged and didn't say anything back. But the man insisted. You know why. She shook her head. Then she owned up to the possibility: okay, how did I die? The man scowled at the fib. Remember the truck? Her face clenched in puzzlement. What truck? Exactly, the man said, his mouth never moving. So Dalia climbed aboard the rope with the man and asked: where am I going? Then she waited at the front desk while the lady there scanned a roster. Oh, that's funny, she said, I don't see you here.

"When I looked," Dalia said, "I see her finger passing over my name. 'So sorry,' she says. 'It looks like our mistake.' I just let them think so. What do you think it all means?"

"Nothing," Boyd said. "You'll live forever."

Then Dalia asked Boyd if he was afraid of dying. He remembered his ex-wife, who believed in heaven. "Of course I am," Boyd said after a minute. "Aren't you? Isn't everyone?"

"Sometimes I think I'm going to die soon. But I'm okay with it." Then she kissed him and said, "I was in the wilderness before I met you."

Then she told Boyd things he didn't want to know about. Dalia told him she heard strange voices, like a radio playing in another room. Sometimes, she lay awake all night long or she'd ride her bicycle in circles around the living room. Once she drove along the coast, closing her eyes as she went into a curve, only opening them as she came out of it. In the sweep of the headlights, she saw the tops of the trees, trudging clumsily up the hillside like sleepwalkers. Dalia laid some heaviness on Boyd. She wept when she wondered what she'd do if her kid died. She told him that when she got pregnant her parents disowned her and the baby's father left her. Then Dalia became a magnet for weirdoes. Men on the street exposed themselves to her. They called her on the phone to tell her what they were doing. At a party, in broad daylight, a guy pushed her head down and unzipped his pants.

"And what did you do," Boyd asked, "did you try stopping him?"

"Don't be angry. It was before I knew you," she said. "I think my brain is at odds with the whole world."

"Oh," Boyd said. He thought of nothing else to say. Then he got angry. He paced the room. He cocked his fist and punched the air. Later Dalia slipped a note to him on faded yellow paper like newsprint: are you mad at me? You don't wanna talk to me. Something like a poem was typed on the reverse side: It's girl. I live it. Yes, but bicycle and don't fall. Don't what I'm OK. I'm very snow. He couldn't understand any of it. But then she came to him, took off her panties and sat in his lap and they watched the sun slip down over the horizon. And over the next several months they became not just physically intimate with each other but emotionally close. She sent him notes, with drawings and song lyrics and dialogue from movies. She cycled with him, fifty miles a day sometimes, and Boyd watched how she cycled up to a drive-through window on her bicycle and angled the mirror on the handlebars to check how she looked, tilting her head back, and Boyd noticed for the first time the fluffy down on her throat that he saw thereafter in certain angles of light. Unconsciously they began dressing alike, wearing the same colors, and Dalia told Boyd they were on the same wavelength. And together they wondered about what had happened to their dreams from when they were kids.

Oh, Dalia: you were something else.

Now Boyd walks down an avenue which cuts diagonally across the street where it happened. There's a market that sells cigarettes and beer, its windows are cluttered with promotions. Boyd hears the electric bus coming and he shudders. After he broke up with Dalia, she coasted down the hill on her mountain bike, the knobby tires like a zipper coming undone. Did she have any inkling of what was going to happen? Boyd planned to go home and watch TV, to do his own thing for a change, and think over how he felt about breaking up with Dalia.

Then he heard a thump. It sounded like a sack of potatoes thudding against the floor. Brake lights flared from a stalled car and he smelled gasoline in the air. Overtaken by a hunch Boyd got closer to the scene of the accident. A white sneaker lay in the road. Then Boyd saw Dalia's bicycle lying tipped over, its handlebars twisted the wrong way. But the bike's tires and rims remained intact. Boyd couldn't look away, he needed to see what had happened. What are you afraid of finding? Nothing. Everything. Then he saw what had happened. Boyd would always see Dalia lying flat on her back in the middle of that street.

"Oh, dear" Boyd thought. What have you done? He didn't know.

He was standing beside her, looking down. Her body sprawled, ponytail fanned above her head, she lay motionless. Had she lost consciousness? She was breathing and didn't look visibly injured, but something was wrong. Was she pulling a prank? Any second, he expected, hoped, for Dalia to pop back up and say: hah, fooled you! An old man with lanky hair wearing cut-offs tapped Boyd's shoulder. The old man clapped a hand over his mouth when he saw Dalia, his hands shaking, legs wobbling, but he kept his footing. Boyd simply sank down and crossed his legs, waiting for the ordeal to end. The crowd of onlookers slinked closer like naughty kids. Then Boyd heard the sirens of emergency vehicles. A black-and-white city cruiser wound its way through the scene. A cop waved the cars off the road. They inched towards the shoulder, making way for the ambulance. A fire engine showed up, a helicopter hovered over the area. After ten minutes, the copter drifted sideways and flew west. Boyd watched the paramedics load her onto a stretcher. She wore a neck brace and had a tube down her throat.

When the officer asked for statements, Boyd told him about their visit to the tower. They'd argued. She'd left him (so to speak). They were breaking up. He was with her, but he didn't see what happened; he only heard it. Boyd didn't know what he was saying. The cop nodded while he took down Boyd's statement. Then the officer told Boyd not to go anywhere. Boyd nodded his head. Boyd listened as the cop asked other witnesses what they had seen. Boyd wasn't hoping for the answer; he was afraid of the answer. Did she veer into traffic on purpose, like somebody stepping in front of a train? The cop was talking to a taxi driver.

"I'm driving," the taxi driver said, "not fast, just the right speed, but she comes right in my way. Hey, I said. Then my taxi knocked her bike away, but she goes upside down high in the air, her feet are trying to step on the ground. Thanks God, I think, I didn't crash her. But then I saw bump when she came down, head smack on the pavement. I remember, my legs locked straight, both feet mashing down the brake, for almost a minute, I sit behind the wheel."

Mouth slack, the man blinks: eyes pure horror.

Boyd gasps for air; for a moment he forgot to breathe. He starts walking up a hill. The sun is a magnifying glass; the air is hot and flat. When he reaches the middle of the slope, a taxi draws up beside him. Boyd wonders what ever happened to the taxi driver that hit Dalia. Boyd hopes he doesn't blame himself. The taxi here now climbs the hill, leaving Boyd behind. Nobody stops for Boyd anymore. You wanted to be alone, he tells himself, now look at you, you are alone. At the next intersection, he watches the approach of a bus and then covers his eyes. If I step in front of the bus, how much will it hurt? What would he feel? Would it be like falling or like he had the wind knocked of him? Would he get dragged along the asphalt, knocked about by the undercarriage? He lets this bus pass. Keep going, he thinks, get away. Now is not the time, here is not the place. When the light changes, he breaks into a jog. The sidewalk takes him down to the water. The sky becomes tender, delicately blue, like a watercolor, under a thin layer of drifting gray cloud. As Boyd passes the yachts at anchor, a cormorant pokes its head in the green water then dives under the surface. A young man in a knit cap and navy blue overalls hoists a cooler into a boat. Cars speed down the 101 highway.

When Boyd reaches the coastal trail, the noises die, and a quiet descends on him, save for the gravel-stones crunching under his feet. A distant sailboat crawls silently along the water in the bay. Boyd sees a tourist dressed in slacks and sneakers take a picture of the cinnamon-colored bridge with a disposable camera. Then Boyd comes to the side of the bluff. The climb is steep. The steps make him stagger. The path tilts up and he kneels suddenly on the wooden retaining edge. The sun's hotness seeps through the foliage. He tips over and lands on the ground. For a minute, he stays down. Boyd pulls himself up, teetering on sore knees. He rises to a half-upright position and thinks about Dalia. They walked these trails and went down along the beach, where they scattered the plovers and picked up sea-glass that was clear, dark brown, green, or blue. Dalia kept their collection in a bowl. Boyd wonders what happened to the pieces.

Boyd waited in the hall outside of Dalia's hospital room, hoping she might wake up. Then a doctor told Boyd that Dalia had died. At first, he felt a kind of relief. The wait was over. There were worse outcomes. He doubted she'd suffered, he hoped she hadn't at any rate. Then the enormity of what had happened settled on him, she was gone, while the world, remorseless, went on without her. Some minutes crept like years; sometimes a whole hour went by in a blink. Nothing went right. Every moment seemed a fight. No day got easier. Sometimes the littlest things affected him: a couple holding hands, talking, sharing a joke. Stay together, he wanted to tell them. Boyd still managed to work. Showed up anyway. Doodled. Made an etching of the penny on a yellow legal pad. Tried to log bugs reported by the beta testers, opened the spreadsheet, watched the blinds knock against the window pane, then he closed the spreadsheet. All the while trying not to cry.

Boyd stayed away from the bridge for a long time, fearful of what he might do. But now he sees the span and he has no plan to jump. He has a plan to walk out on the bridge to prove he can resist the urge. The parking lot is full. A white coach, angled at the curb, disembarks tourists. They make for the round gift shop with the plate-glass windows. The air feels cool but the sun's rays singe Boyd's face. People are everywhere, they take pictures; nobody notices Boyd walking right by them, squinting. He takes the street under the bridge; he can hear the tires slapping the spacers overhead. The air smells of exhaust fumes. When he reaches the other side, he climbs the ramp towards the bridge. On your left, somebody says: a mountain bike makes a ratcheting sound. He knows this side is for cyclists, not pedestrians. But this is the right side for

Boyd. If he can make it to the second tower before the police or park rangers force him to turn back, he will stand over the spot where Dalia's ashes were dispersed.

Boyd steps on the walkway. Though he can hear the surf boom and the spray crashing, the water between the bluffs and the headlands becomes a calm green puddle. The wind backs off. The air feels almost muggy. Seemingly in no time he reaches the first tower. Out here, the wind blows keenly. A few feet away, barely the length of his arm, a gull floats on an updraft, so close Boyd thinks of reaching out and touching the bird's wings. He gazes upward at the tower. From this vantage point, the tower seems short, not big at all, it's not golden either, but reddish-brown. There are signs on the tower: No Littering: $1000 Fine. Another sign has a phone number, asking if you are troubled, you should call. Boyd thinks how easily he could make the jump. All he needs to do is throw his leg over the rail and let the rest of him follow: so quick nobody would notice. A truck thunders by and the walkway trembles. Now a hatchback speeds past him: a face behind steamed glass.

He reaches the halfway point of the bridge, where the fog comes down. Now he sees himself standing in the lee of the second tower. Boyd remembers how Dalia kept him from meeting her family, until one day her father showed up unannounced at her apartment, and Dalia let the old man come inside and Boyd met him. Her father didn't stay, said he had things to do.

"You two have fun now," he said, "okay?"

When her father left, she led him to the living room. Boyd kissed her lying on the carpet, as open-mouthed as two birds feeding each other. She stood, fanned herself, then walked towards the mattress. She made a joke of dragging her feet, saying: "do I want this, I don't know, I think I do." Then Boyd undressed her. He remembers the sight of her abdomen going up and down, and when he removed his boxers, she said: "good lord, maybe you could do it while I watch." She shrieked with laughter.

Following Dalia's death, her family had her body cremated. Boyd was asked to come along, it was what Dalia would have wanted, her mother said, and Boyd could tell they had no idea that he'd just broken up with her when the accident happened. He didn't tell them the truth. He thought they still needed him, Boyd was their last connection to Dalia. So he joined them on the dock across the bay, where together they boarded a small cabin cruiser. They went to this cove past the headlands and beyond the bridge, the engine churning the water. Boyd tossed red rose petals over the side of the boat and the captain circled the spot where the petals floated three times. Pinching her collar together, Dalia's mother climbed out of the cabin, trailed by Dalia's father. Their stocky bearded pastor, from their small plain church in the avenues, emerged last of all. The mother hugged the bag of ashes; the father talked to the bag of ashes. The pastor said he knew how much Dalia loved the ocean. They were giving her to the whole world, he said, to the earth itself. They took turns dispersing the yellow-gray ashes, scattering the soft sift among the rose petals. When the bag was empty, the captain told them about the burial rites at sea and everybody stood while he rang the bell. Slowly the pastor leafed through the pages of his bible. The words squeezed into Boyd's head, become weighted, and knocked together inside him. The pastor was talking about being guided by love, about being kind and patient, about being happy when goodness prevails, and wanting the best for everyone.

"You all know this chapter," the pastor said. "They read it at weddings." He suddenly swung his arm as the boat pitched in a slight swell. "So what does it mean for us today?" He stared at a place beyond them. "With love, we are always ready to forgive. With love, we can accept whatever may come our way, and with love, we will endure it, no matter how terrible."

The pastor let those words sink in. Dalia's mother didn't say anything. The pastor shook his head at Boyd. Boyd felt sure the man knew everything, as if Boyd had confessed everything with the look on his face. But the pastor only posed a question to all of them, saying: "will you love, will you let love be your guide?"

The mother nodded vigorously, the father clasped his hands, and then they all looked at Boyd. The truth was he'd always felt uncomfortable with outwards shows of religiosity. It seemed like they wanted to hold his hand and say a prayer together, to make a vow of some kind. Boyd heard himself start to say something. "I don't know." He mumbled something about the break-up. Nobody seemed to catch his words. "I don't know," he said again. The parents looked at each other, their faces uneasy. Sensing something was amiss, the pastor glanced away from Boyd and looked at the family members sitting with their feet planted as the boat rocked and then stared back at Boyd.

"Well, let me ask you again. Will you love?" When the mother frowned at him Boyd looked at the pastor and saw his eyes pleading with him to answer wisely.

A cough clawed Boyd's throat. "I hope so," Boyd's old self said. "I hope I still can."

Forty minutes later, Boyd's new self thinks, what am I doing here? But he is pretty sure he knows. The fog is a shroud. He throws a leg over the railing and sits on top, both knees up. Out here, the wind pushes him back, pinning him against the rails. He sips the air through his nose. "I miss you," he says. Something seems to brush past him. "Are you here? It feels like it." Then he shakes his head. His consciousness flickers. He can barely string a thought together. His mind seems to step, pause, look both ways, and then cautiously take another step forward. He wants to stop so he can think. He needs to explain something. He thinks of writing a note, of walking away, but now he is lowering his legs and bracing his heels. He is staring down as waves break on the pier foundation, the crests curling white like metal shavings. I just want to stay here for a minute. He tries to think; he tries not to think. He lowers his head. There's no stopping now.

He retrieves the penny from his pocket and rubs the coin between his thumb and forefinger, then holds the penny with both hands a few inches from his face. He is unsure what he is going to do, but then he knows, it is simple, like making a wish or saying a prayer, and he throws the penny into the bay. Tumbling, spinning, the penny makes a brief speck in the air. It flies away. The penny is gone below, disappearing where the water breaks. He doesn't feel any different. He'd thought maybe getting rid of the penny might lift the hex or jinx, or whatever it was, and ward off the karma. All right, Boyd says to himself, now I know. He's read about jumpers. From this height, they usually die from the impact: like falling on cement. But some survive the fall then drown. A person might plunge as much as forty feet below the surface. All these thoughts scramble through his mind. When there is nothing left, he releases his grip. He sees himself throw his body out and do a swan dive. Oh, hey, he says. He is grappling with the sky, reaching, trying to turn. His fingers snatch and grab for the railing but he is still going down, he's too far over, and he thinks he hears bicycles go by. He feels the wind shoving him, grabbing him, and his hands are gripping the girder while his legs swing freely under the bridge. He is hanging by his fingertips, suspended and dangling limply over the ocean. Somehow he has caught hold of a girder. Every which way, he is struggling, his biceps quivering. Beneath the bridge, the wind rushes, flaps in his ears, a dull and monotonous roar. Fierce gusts pummel him, buffeting him back, I can't fight this wind. His nose begins to drip, tears gather in his eyes. He wants to cup his palms and muffle his poor ears. He never knew he weighed so much. His legs seem filled with gravel. His whole body jerks back and forth. The motion is wearing out his arms. But then Boyd becomes clever, realizing he is going to get out of this, he has to pull himself up. Pain is stabbing his upper arms. His neck is cramping. He rouses himself, works himself up. His torso begins to lift slightly. Now his eyes are level with the girder.

Keep going, a little more, almost there. But then he sinks back down and he is looking up at the girder. His shoulder-blades feel ready to poke through his back. Okay, don't stop this time. Now it is as if he is climbing up a rope, hand over hand, and he digs his chin into the girder between a pair of rivets. He struggles and using his muscles swings himself up onto the girder. He is lying still on the girder letting his body recover by degrees.

Boyd performs a kind of systems-check, a scan of his limbs. An arm hangs down; his head lolls; his legs stick to the girder. Even with sore ears, he hears the surf smash the rocks beneath the bridge. He can smell the water: salt-tinged air, brine, kelp and rocks. The wind snatches at his pants and tugs at the sleeves of his windbreaker. He is thinking: am I hurt? The fatigue is settling in. He tries to say something. Without warning, his face puckers and his eyes water; hand clamped over his mouth, he sobs, weeps. It gives way to a wailing that lasts for several minutes.

"Okay now," he says. Breathe. Stand up. Get moving. Slowly, like a shadow detaching itself from the ground, he climbs to his feet. He moves away from the edge. The cold pours over him, his ears ache, and he rubs his palms together for warmth. Painful memories shyly tuck themselves away. Seagulls fly overhead and kids skip along the walkway. Boyd lifts a foot, hops onto the walkway. He gazes at the rooftops on the hills. He makes out the tower nestled in the trees, like something from years ago, and he laughs about today. Well, look at that, he thinks. Then: hey everybody, watch me. Here I am walking back towards the city.

NOBODY'S TOWN

You'd see him at the coffee house, shuffling pages of typescript, broad-shouldered, with thick black hair, eating a baguette. Local literary magazines printed Matt Vogler's stories in loosely stapled pamphlets with lopsided pages. He wrote a twelve-story cycle about people from youth to middle age in flight from the past, hoping their journey would shed the long-ago person everybody remembered. The book was named *Telling Tales of Our Time* and Matt repeated the title, the words leaping off his tongue. Then he landed an agent. There was interest from several small presses. In the bookstore, the floor creaking, Matt would linger in the aisle and look at the spines to see which authors would share the V shelf with him. This is love, Matt thought, I am in love with the whole world. Closing his eyes, he pictured rows of people listening to him reading. He saw them stand, clap, and form lines to see him while he sat at a table signing books.

But the moment of truth had come: Who am I kidding? I'm no writer, no writer-writer. Who was he but a nobody? Once upon a time, when he was 28, Matt believed in himself. His writing was burgeoning, he was at the peak of his capabilities, on the cusp of a breakthrough. He was building a local following. But then something happened, or rather, nothing happened. No publisher accepted the manuscript. The editors advised him to publish in periodicals with a heftier literary cachet. So Matt sent his stories in large goldenrod envelopes, using rolls of stamps in the process. He became a regular at the post office. He received a pro forma rejection slip for each submission. Then he punched holes in the rejection letter and put it in a three-ring looseleaf binder.

Somewhere around the age of 39 Matt realized he had stopped writing, his stories hung in folders in a metal filing cabinet. The world, it seemed, would hear nothing more from him. In public, on the bus, at a street corner, or in a store, a person sometimes frowned at him. "I forget your name," he or she would say, "but I remember your story, like a two-thousand-word haiku. Who are you again?" "Nobody, really," Matt would answer, "I teach writing; I'm an instructor." He became too old for dreams anymore, somehow he lost momentum, got sidetracked. The magic went away. The lack of money got him down. Matt's big break never came. He had no connections. He settled down, telling himself that the odds apply to everybody. His life could have been worse. Matt grew up in a town nobody knew and started out with nothing. When he turned thirteen, his mom got sick: cancer. She died one morning while he rode his paper route. Dad disappeared and the fridge gathered past due notices. The utilities to his house were cut so Matt showered in the locker room and sprayed his shirts with cologne. When his classmates applied to college, he worked odd jobs: mowed the football field, weeded soybeans, detasseled corn, pumped gas at the filling station. Half his wages went into his VW beetle. It was an old stick-shift, vanilla-yellow, rust-scabbed, with paperback books scattered on the seat. He'd drive to the quarry and stare at the water or take the blacktop to the highway and watch the cars go by.

When the army recruiter called, Matt told him he wanted Europe. Six months later, he landed in West Germany. A two-year stint stretched to three, then four. He went places, saw things, got away when he could. He traveled. He read. He picked up German, a smattering of French, Spanish, he could get by in Greek. It was all so unlikely, he thought. When he returned stateside, he headed out to San Francisco. After three years, he entered Berkeley, where he wrote papers comparing Chaucer, Petrarch, and Boccaccio. Following graduation, he taught English at a language institute, while doing an MFA in creative writing at USF. Then City College offered him a year-long appointment for an instructor on sabbatical. The sabbatical became sick-leave, then the instructor died. They encouraged him to apply: a year-long, full-time, renewable contract. The position was his if he wanted it. He took the job, what else could he do? That was nine years ago already. The city became home.

The job too had its pleasures. Matt had his own

cubicle and he got free books for consideration for use in classes. When they assigned courses, he finagled an afternoon schedule to have his mornings free. The students asked Matt if he was still writing? Everything was chaos, he told his classes, when he went too long without writing. He wrote to get even with life, as if to say, I am not beaten. Sometimes Matt's philosophy clicked with a student and Matt took care to mark that student's story, wringing the syntax until each sentence tightened into a knot. Of course he was still writing, he always was, not writing was too terrible to contemplate. What was he working on? He was reworking *Telling Tales of Our Time*. Cutting and pasting from the drafts, he made a paragraph of clean copy, then another. When would he publish? Talent only helped so much, that was just reality. Writing took time. Luck played its role too. But Matt told his students to write whether their work was published or not. You need to have faith. Frowning, the students shuffled away, looking as if they wanted to scrub their hands.

Matt dragged himself clumsily out of bed every morning. He guarded this private time jealously and wrote for an hour before he brewed a pot of coffee, before the doubts had time to work on him and told him to quit. The words came to him quietly, faintly, wisps moving at tiptoe speed. When Matt began to type in his head he heard the beautiful words in his stories, but anyone else listening would hear the click-clack, clickety-clack, of his keyboard. He would chuckle to himself as the letters ran across the monitor's screen, and sometimes he'd catch himself mouthing the words as he typed. He scrolled up and down, cutting and pasting his paragraphs until they stood in the right order. Then he saved his work to a diskette.

Matt began each day this way until this morning. At five a.m., he sat, slump-shouldered, at his desk. On a good day, he worked through anything; today was not a good day. He sloshed the coffee over this tongue. The phone rang in the corner, the bell clattering shrilly, breaking the silence in his office. The noise startled him. He plugged his ears while the cursor blinked sullenly at him from the computer screen. Wrong number, he thought, had to be. Nobody ever called; who could be calling so early? I'm not answering, no way am I answering. Now is my writing time. But the phone kept ringing.

"Shush," he said under his breath. "Hush. Be quiet. Stop calling me."

He stared at the monitor and highlighted a sentence in the story he was working on. He tapped the delete key. Scrolling the page, he forgot where he left off, forgot where he was, what he was doing, his mind wandered. He didn't know what to do next. Was this writer's block? He felt his memory leak, like an oil pan loosely plugged. The characters dripped and dribbled out, leaving hardly a spot. He clawed the keyboard. Write something bad, he told himself. A kind of frantic inertia took hold of him: he needed to do something but he couldn't think of anything to do. His head felt like a tire stuck with a nail, leaking air. Matt got to his feet and the phone rang again, as if his movement had somehow made the caller dial again.

A minute later, his wife Deana stood, yawning, in the doorway. "Who called?"

He shrugged. "Nobody, as far as I know."

She checked the answering machine. "Maybe it was important."

"I was trying to work."

They made the bed like strangers, barely speaking. In the bathroom, she sang a song then hummed when she forgot the words. As Deana took a shower, Matt got dressed, tucking his shirt into his jeans, pairing it with a tweed jacket. He stuffed the Gogol paperback into his breast pocket and gathered the students' papers. He left a note for Deana. I'll be marking papers in my office all afternoon, submitting grade sheets. As he printed his name, the phone rang again and he ignored it.

As he unlocked his office, Matt stepped over the students' papers scattered over the carpet. He stacked them on his desk. Then a steady flow of students came to his office. One kid shook Matt's hand; he enjoyed the class, even though it was English. The next student, goggle-eyed, laid her paper down wordlessly. The last guy apologized for the faint ink of his print-out. When the entrances became sporadic, Matt shut the door and skimmed the papers. Few had reached the ten-page requirement. Most amounted to eight. Several barely broke past the sixth page. One breached a twelfth page. As per usual, the paper looked like a five-paragraph theme stretched to fill up those dozen pages: long meandering paragraphs lacking any trace of an argumentative edge. In the margins, Matt penciled a cursive note on the last page then sorted the papers into four stacks and assigned grades to them. These papers wouldn't change anybody's final grade that Matt could see. Then the office phone rang. It tootled like a mischievous flute that made Matt's eye twitch. He shut the door to his cubicle before picking up the phone.

"Hello, Mr. Vogler's office. It's me." There was a split-second delay, and his voice echoed at the other end of the line.

"Mr. Vogler, I mean Matthew or Matt, if I may?" The caller spoke with a twang.

"Who's calling?" Matt watched a paper slide under the door.

"Corey Welch," the woman said. "You met me once when you were a kid."

"I don't remember you." Then he added: "Corey, are you sure?"

"Nobody answered when I called the home number. I thought about leaving a message. Then I realized I forgot about the time difference. I wasn't even sure I had the right number."

"I heard the phone ringing."

"Did I wake you? Oh, I'm sorry."

"No, I was busy, doing something."

"I'm so relieved. I thought you moved and nobody knew where. But I knew about the college and they gave me your number and somehow now I've got through to you."

"I guess you're lucky. You might've missed me altogether. The semester ended today. I'm only here a few hours. I was getting ready to leave. Then we're off for five weeks." Matt yawned, putting a fist up to his mouth.

Corey was a nurse, calling Matt long distance from the hospital in Fairbury, about his father. His father's health was seriously failing, he had a weak heart and had one of his kidneys removed. Now Matt's father had pneumonia and nobody thought he'd last the winter.

"Yesterday he said get my son on the phone and tell him about the situation. Get him out here before it's too late."

"What can I do?" Matt asked. "My dad never cared about me. He never cared about anybody. He never cared even about himself."

"He almost died. He's staying in the hospital. He's under observation."

"So he's on the mend."

"Officially, I think so. They will probably discharge him in a day or two, three on the outside. His condition is serious but I see worse all the time. It's his demeanor that has me worried. He mopes. He stares out the window. When I look, there's nobody there. You have to come home. He needs you."

"It's the holiday season," Matt said. "I don't think I can. The flights will all be booked."

"I knew your mother," she said, continuing as if she had anticipated everything Matt might say. "She was a patient here when I started, twenty-five years ago. She'd want you to come."

"She'd want a lot of things. She'd want to know all about what happened."

Matt remembered being 13 years old, standing at his mother's gravesite in winter, red scraped-looking cheeks, corn stalks, frozen ground.

"You're all he has," Corey was saying. "He doesn't have much. He just wants to see you, before it's too late, because, well, you know."

Matt shook his head then switched ears. "I can

check the flights." He tapped the switch hook. There goes the semester break. While he was leaving his office the department chair approached him and waved a sheet of paper at him. "I have your spring schedule." Matt couldn't look at the paper now. He didn't care. Right now he wanted to leave the building and never come back or ever teach again. He'd probably get sick now. Everybody was sick. His body knew the semester was over, the work was done, and he could fall apart for a while.

"Is everything all right?" The department chair asked, and she cringed slightly as if somebody had shouted in her ear.

Matt told her a little about his father, about his childhood and the town. She nodded. She understood. She knew all about staring at the cars on the freeway, watching them go by, and thinking about how getting away must feel, to hit the road, to go anywhere. And the town: corn stalks, rows of soybeans, train tracks, grain elevators, gravel driveways, houses sagging on their foundations. Rusted hulks of scrapped autos, farm implements, scratchy weed patches. The summer hot, like a furnace with gnats, the winter's unstinting coldness.

"That's the place exactly," Matt said.

"He must be proud: you, a college instructor, loved by students, a natural teacher."

"Sometimes I have wondered."

She looked at him curiously. "Lucky I caught you. Some news: should have a tenure-track opening in the spring. Keep this quiet, but I'm encouraging you to submit your application."

"Well, thanks," Matt said. "Yes. Definitely, thanks a lot. I will think about it."

Matt dressed in dark blue corduroy trousers, a striped cotton shirt, and a gray herringbone jacket. He packed his computer, which was the size of a thick pizza box, in his suitcase, along with its power cable, mouse, and keyboard. There was room for little clothing, but he had to take his computer despite the hassle, so he could write. The monitor sat in its carton, taped shut, and wrapped with twine for carrying. Kneeling before the bookcase, he stared at the spines and took *The Maltese Falcon*, *On the Road*, and *Cannery Row* off the shelf and stuffed them in his pockets. He didn't know why. Read so long ago, they'd meant something to him once. He was standing at the front window when Deana slipped her hand under his elbow and rested her palm on his chest.

"I wish I could tag along," she said.

"Why, whatever for?"

"See where you come from. You seem like this orphan I barely know."

"I booked the ticket already. Besides, you'd hate everything there."

"You're not embarrassed by me, are you?"

He shook his head. "I'm embarrassed by him." Matt looked at Deana and held her tight. "Some other time," he said. "If he pulls through, maybe we can go in the summer." A car horn honked in the street. Deana looked out the window.

"The shuttle van's here," she said.

"All right," Matt said to himself as the plane took off, "let's show him who we are."

But when the plane touched down, the dreary landscape punched him in the stomach. The cold, he'd forgotten the bitter demoralizing chill of sub-zero midwestern air, how it actually felt. It burrowed into his herringbone jacket, his corduroys did nothing to stop the freezing and his skin tingled numbly. It was as if his body was shutting down. He was sure his blood became so thick and sluggish that his heart actually beat more slowly. In the arrivals hall, people were gathered, waiting for loved ones. A teenage girl with a bloated stomach sprawled on the bench, reading a paperback. A custodian dozed standing up by a column. Then Matt went outside. The air smelled of diesel fumes, but the bus to the car rental lot had the heater blowing full blast, and Matt stopped shivering and felt a little warmed up by the time the bus reached the car rental agency.

When the service rep saw Matt, lugging his suitcase and the monitor box, the man waved a clipboard at the window.

"With the wind chill," the man said, "it's probably fifteen below out there."

"I thought I could manage," Matt said. He set down the box on the floor and stood close to it.

"Car's coming up in a minute," the service rep said. The man immediately hunched over a stack of papers, a cramped-looking hand against his forehead. He kept sniffling. He walked out from behind the counter, stuck out his head. In worn-down shoes, he stamped his feet and paced around the box, chin sunk in his chest.

. "What's inside here," he asked, "a microwave?"

Then a white four-door stopped outside, salt-dusted tires, icicles under the bumper. As Matt drove snow drifted along the dark road and flakes floated against the windshield. By early afternoon he arrived in farming country. Extending for miles, the white fields bristled with broken stalks. Long gravel driveways ended at a two-story house with a peaked roof. Beside each barn there stood a concrete silo with a dome. Vines crawled up the staves and the iron hoops dribbled rust. After two hours, Matt swung the car off the interstate and followed the old highway route. A driver waved, two fingers rising from the steering wheel. Matt remembered this town now. But when the corner came, he missed the turn and braked on the shoulder. With the engine idling, he sat for a few minutes, adjusted the rear-view mirror and switched off the engine. He wanted to write something, to say something about what was happening inside him, but nothing came to him except for what he was seeing. He thought of reading a paragraph. He sat so long his hands became cold, his breath visible. Finally, he started the car and drove, under the speed limit, to the hospital to see his father.

Matt arrived at the hospital, parked his car, and walked upstairs, going directly to the nurse's station. He gave them his name and when he asked if Nurse Corey worked today, the woman behind the desk nodded energetically. Matt sat down and tried to read. He worried about his computer, wondering if the trip or the cold had damaged anything. He thought about writing something. What can I write now about this moment? He listed the things in the room: a mangled venetian blind, a knotted cord, the lucite rental-car tab with a cable holding the keys. Then somebody called his name, the voice from the phone. Matt stuck a thumb between the pages. A stout woman wearing powder-blue scrubs stood before him.

"I have good news," she said. "The doctor signed his discharge paper."

"How did you know who I was?"

"Nobody else is here." She looked at him squarely. "But I recognized you. Uncanny, a lot like your mom, I bet you remind him of her."

Matt felt his face empty and he glanced away. Inside the room a nurse's aide wearing a surgeon's mask was stripping a mattress. She rolled up the sheet and tossed the bundle into a canvas-sided laundry cart. When Matt stepped forward, Nurse Corey grasped his wrist. "He's packing. How about something to drink in the meantime? Would you like coffee, water, or soda-pop? Some juice?"

"I could do with a cup of water," Matt replied.

She poured water into a paper cup and when he gulped the whole drink, she said: "I guess you were pretty thirsty."

"I didn't know what to expect," he said. "I thought maybe I'd be on a death-watch. I didn't even call ahead to reserve a room anywhere. I thought I'd be here."

"It's great news," Nurse Corey said, "in fact, it's nearly miraculous. Nobody expected him to recover, so completely, we were all surprised."

Matt crumpled the cup after he'd finished drinking

the water inside and walked to his father's room with the nurse. The door stood ajar but the nurse knocked before stepping inside. The blinds were up and the sun brought out the reddish tint in Nurse Corey's swept-back hair, dyed the color of an old tarnished penny. His father stood at the bed, staring at the TV, cheerful blue eyes in a sagging, grumpy face. Matt glanced at the screen. They were playing *Cannery Row*, and Matt watched Doc lying on a cot toss up an orange and then Matt saw the orange drop back into Doc's hand again.

"Is that him? You're here," Matt's father said, "what took you so long?"

The old man stood wearing a pair of shorts and shoes that had no laces. His feet looked swollen. His shins had scaly patches, and purplish welts showed beneath the skin. He shambled forward and clutched Matt in a hug, pawing his upper arms, his stomach solid as a boulder. He smelled of bleached linen.

"It's been a while," he said: "too much time." He held Matt by the biceps. His grimy hands needed washing. "How long has it been?"

"Twelve years, I'd say."

The old man stared at Matt, his mouth slightly gaping. "Don't wait so long next time."

When Matt didn't reply, the old man grinned, revealing his yellowing teeth, what was left of them.

"What happened to the teeth?"

"Oh, them?" he huffed, breathing through his mouth. "Teaching the neighbor kid how to swing a baseball bat. Hit me in the mouth. Not the nose, thank goodness, missed the nose."

He plopped a hand on his belly and blew out his

breath. Blinking, he looked ready to doze off right then.

"Are you ready to go home?" Corey asked.

His face twitched; he was trying to say something, his lips nudging along words nobody could make out. "Yeah," he said, whispering hoarsely. "I'm ready to go home. Let's go."

Matt walked beside Corey as she wheeled the old man down the corridor. When Matt brought the car up, he bumped his head while getting into the car and winced. He was completely out of breath. Corey eased the door shut after Matt's old man was safely inside.

"You two stay out of trouble now," she said.

The old man rolled down the window. He was gasping, and his hands trembled. "Don't do anything I wouldn't do," he said. He wiped his nose with the back of his hand.

The alarm clock rang in the next bedroom and woke Matt up. Why hadn't his father turned off the alarm? What if he has died? What will I do? He quickly went to his father's bedroom and knocked on the door.

"Dad? It's Matt. Are you all right?" When he didn't get a response Matt opened the door and saw his father's belly rising and falling under the sheet. The alarm clock fell on the floor and the ringing ceased. Nobody said anything for a minute.

"Tired," the old man said, "give me a few minutes."

Matt took a shower of hard lukewarm water before unpacking his suitcase. He liberated his computer from his suitcase and set it up with the monitor at his old desk. He stared at the blank computer screen, waiting for inspiration. Speak to me, will you? Say something.

Nothing came. He wanted to write, same as every morning, he came ready to work, but when he sat down, nothing happened. He tried reading a student's story but it seemed awful. He flipped through the pages hoping to find something salvageable, to no avail, so he sat there shuffling the sheets of paper. Matt heard the boards creak and saw the old man standing in the door frame. He'd lost an inch or two of height, his face was pale, and his clothing hung loosely from his body.

"Seems awfully early," the old man said. "I didn't think you'd be awake until noon, at the earliest."

"I woke up at six. I get up early every morning."

The old man squinted at the computer on the desk. "You lugged that thing here?"

"For my writing," Matt said, "first thing every morning. I feel awful if I skip it."

"What do you write about?"

Matt tried to explain. He wrote stories about characters who had epiphanies but ignored them, shirking their significance.

"I'm reworking my stuff," he said: "I just tell myself, go, type. One rule: never write a story about a writer writing a story."

"I wish I wrote," his father said. "But now it's too late. I'd like to read something of yours."

"Sure, why not?"

After a minute, Matt shut down the machine and they went downstairs. The old man said he needed to get to work and asked Matt for a lift into town.

"You just got out of the hospital."

"Nobody is running the station. You can help me. You work the pumps and I'll ring up the sales." He sat at the table and pulled on a pair of shabby boots. "This old man's got to get a buck together somehow."

"What about some breakfast?"

"I made a plan for that too. There's a coffee shop next door to the station."

"We don't need to go out for breakfast. Let me toast some of the sourdough. Brew some coffee. Fry some eggs." He swung open the fridge, took in the empty shelf, and stepped back.

The old man's face wrinkled and he shook his head. "No, I told myself yesterday first thing tomorrow I'll show him the town. It's diversified. You should see the gas station."

"I know what a gas station looks like."

"We expanded, rebuilt, cleaned up. The owner renovated the coffee shop, added a food mart, gift store, tourist information booth."

"What do you need with all that, what gifts, what tourist information?"

"You'd be surprised. We get all kinds of visitors now. Train buffs come to see the site where the wreck took place. They shop for antiques. They travel old Route 66."

After putting on a coat, Matt and his father got in the car. Starting the engine, Matt could see the whole of their property, just on the shoulder of the town road. We always lived on the outskirts, he told himself, where the houses stop and the fields begin. Halfway down the driveway, he stepped on the brake pedal, the tires gripping the packed dirt, looking at the things he'd missed last night in the dark. They'd cut down the oak tree but left the stump at the edge of the lawn. His neighbor's field was now a construction site. There was a mound of dirt, littered with clods of soil, chunks of concrete, field stones, and on top stood a motorcycle. A chain fence puffed in the wind, the links jangling.

Matt shook his head. "What were they building?"

"An apartment complex," the old man said. "It's not finished."

"It looks abandoned. They stop for the winter?"

"No. Somebody was there the other day. They work year round. They sweep the snow out. They're going to build three more units."

He pointed at the plywood molds holding the concrete for the foundation.

"You ever work construction?" Matt's father asked. "I always wanted to, I like working with my hands. I might see maybe they can use an old coot like me for something. When they dug the hole, I blinked all the time for all the dust stinging my face."

Matt saw his father as the young man he remembered, a man who could knock in a nail with two strikes of a hammer.

"This developer wants to buy our land too," the old man said, staring into the woods.

"What did you tell them?"

"Nothing, I haven't made up my mind yet. Maybe I will. Probably should."

As they passed their neighbor's yard Matt noticed a sign on a tree that read: Tow Away No Stopping Anytime. Matt thought that would be a good title for a story. Nobody wrote much about construction workers, they were a vanishing part of American culture. But they might have the makings of a pretty good story.

Meanwhile, the old man did some talking. Of course, he had thought about leaving. "I wanted to leave when your mother died," he said. "So many days, I stared at the blacktop, watching the eighteen-wheelers heading away, and I wanted to hop aboard and drive somewhere, anywhere, maybe head down south or out west, anyplace where the weather stayed warm during the winter."

Matt frowned when they arrived at his father's gas station. Spools of black-ribbed plastic tubing, five-foot high, filled the lot behind the building. They looked to be the same spools as twelve years ago, if not twenty. As he pulled into the lot of the filling station, Matt drove over the pink air-hose and heard the bell clink in the maintenance bay. At the other end was the diner. In the window Matt watched a waitress wipe her hands down on her apron and saw wide-backed men in caps and quilted vests swivel round as Matt parked the car with his father. A man in square wire-rimmed glasses touched a finger to the bill of his cap, and then everybody turned back to the counter. Sitting in the passenger seat, the old man crossed his arms over his paunch. Something seemed to flicker in his eyes; then he clenched his jaw. "I wanted to be a good father. I tried to straighten you out the way my old man straightened me out. I know I wasn't a good father. But I wanted to be. The intent was there."

Matt gripped the wheel and didn't reply. What could he say? I don't want to know, Matt told himself: don't drag us backwards into a life that ended long ago.

"Well, yeah, I guess it's tough." But Matt thought: you're why I never wanted kids: what if I turned out like you? "Anyway," Matt said then let his voice trail off. He didn't want to talk about this.

"So you understand me better, we're all right?"

"Yeah, we're okay."

The old man swung the door open and plopped out his leg. "I'm glad you came. Too bad you didn't bring the girl." He coughed, hacking, and snuffed his nose.

"It's still holiday time, and they're totally busy at the store."

"Who shops after Christmas?"

"Some people wait for the clearance sales. She'd miss out on the commissions."

Matt held the door open while the old man shuffled to a table by the cash register. The diner's aroma was that of coffee percolating mixed with the smell of cigarette smoke. Matt remained on his feet while the waitress wiped the table, then he sat down. Now Matt smelled toasted bread and bacon sizzling on a hot oiled griddle. The old man ordered his "usual"; the waitress scribbled on the guest check. Then Matt asked for a poached egg, toasted wheat bread, and a cup of coffee. The coffee had slick spots on top and tasted slightly of dish soap. When the waitress brought the food, the old man knifed a dollop of butter on the top pancake, then soaked the stack with maple syrup, letting it flow down the sides and into the sausage links. In the kitchen, the cook hollered when each order was ready: Sunnyside! Over easy! Scrambled! When the waitress replenished the coffee, she looked at Matt and asked him where he came from. Matt didn't have time to answer. The old man blurted out: "he's my son, he's from here." Then he nudged Matt. "She's new to the town. Couple years now, am I right or am I right?"

The waitress ignored Matt's father. "You don't look like a local," she said, gazing at Matt.

"I live out in California now." .

She nodded and the trucker at the next table clinked a quarter on the saucer. The waitress watched the trucker go while she shook a squirt-bottle of ketchup for fullness.

"He's paying a visit to his old man before he kicks the bucket," Matt's father said, after a few seconds.

"I always wanted to tour California," the waitress said. "You ever see any movie stars?"

"They're all down in L.A. I live up north, in San Francisco."

"Whoa, San Fran," she said. "How do you like living out there in Frisco."

Matt said nothing. When she flinched, he figured he looked disappointed. "I'm sorry," he said. "Nobody says 'Frisco.' It's not a dirty word. But only tourists say it. People will look at you funny."

"What do you call it out there?"

"We just say the city."

"What city?" the old man said. "Chicago is the city. They should call it the town."

"That's what we say for Oakland: we call it the town. Oaktown."

She turned away from Matt's father and knitted her brows. "You sure he's your dad?"

"Yes, I am. Pretty sure, unless they lied to me."

"I always thought he was making you up, I never believed he had a son. I am sorry."

Matt became puzzled. "I don't understand."

"I'm sorry for you," the waitress said. "You're stuck with him as your old man." She made a face that wasn't nice, a kind of sneer.

When she left, the old man growled, loud enough for the waitress to hear. "Never mind her," he said, "I never could figure out what makes her so rude and spiteful. A spoilt child."

When the waitress laid the check on the table, the old man reached around himself and came up empty-handed. He patted himself down. He started coughing. When he said he'd left his wallet at home, Matt looked at the waitress's bored face and he pulled out his wallet and put the money down on the table. She led him to the cash register with its nickel-sized keys. She counted out Matt's change while he read the advertisement on the counter. It said The Flavor of Adventure. In the picture, a brawny man with a craggy face straddled a rock, holding a puck-sized container of tobacco. The words burned inside his eyelids. See. Remember. Save for later.

Matt stood beside the cash register in the gas station for about an hour before anyone showed up, while the old man rested in a chair. They both watched the road, neither one of them said anything for a long time. Matt told the old man about the gas stations in the city, how they had booths with thick glass and an intercom, and when you wanted gas, you had to pay first by putting the money in the pay-drawer, and tell the cashier which pump to authorize. Sometimes cars even lined up and you had to wait a long time for your turn. They sure didn't have that problem here. Nope.

Then, plodding along the loop of road, a Winnebago appeared and lurched into the lot, pulling in next to the pumps island. The old man glanced at the vehicle confusedly, squinting, with a scowl, as if from disbelief. Then his mind wandered back to the present.

"That's the first customer of the day out there," the old man said, "better beat feet, shoo!"

The driver tooted the horn and Matt knocked on the window: "fill'er up?"

The driver nodded. Matt blew into his hands and turned the gas tank cap until it huffed a gasp of air then he inserted the nozzle and set the catch so he didn't have to hold the trigger. While the pump clicked off the gallons, Matt sniffed at the fumes and watched the pink air hose hiss on the concrete slab. The driver tapped the windshield and Matt left the nozzle and sponged the windshield with the cleaner before swiping the glass with the squeegee. He watched their lips move and began to make out the words. He wanted to ask the people in the camper about their trip, but he said nothing. The nozzle clanked and he hung it back up and took the money, counted the change, and handed the receipt to the driver, who tipped him a dollar. The Winnebago shuddered away, teetering through the reflector poles. The vehicle slowly straightened on the blacktop then headed for the old highway route.

Matt was washing his hands at the basin when the phone rang. The old man barely moved. Matt picked up the phone.

"I wanted to check in with you," Nurse Corey said over the line. "I tried the house but nobody answered. How's he holding up?"

"He wanted to work today."

"I would like to talk to him. Can I talk to him?"

"He fell asleep in his chair. Snoring. Looks fine."

"How are you, are you two getting along?"

Matt rubbed his knuckles. The skin was dry and painful as if he was developing a rash. He wanted to tell her that the sight of the old man affected him severely, because he looked so unhealthy. "I am all right. He talks my ear off."

"When I told him you were coming, he clammed up. He worried about how things looked. 'I'm nobody,' he said, 'I never became anybody.' But he takes great pride in you."

"Yeah, he wants to take the credit, trying to build himself up."

"He's embarrassed. He needs to think he did something right."

But things were better. His father's bitterness and resentment at life had faded, and Matt's ill feelings towards his father had diminished. The old man seemed to accept how his life turned out. When the call ended, Matt dialed the number for his apartment in San Francisco. Deana didn't answer.

While Matt was visiting his father the weather warmed up. Ice melted in the ditches. A mesh of fog lay on the ground. Then the sun unlocked the top soil and the air smelled of thawing wood. Birds, most likely crows, made silent specks in the sky. Somebody was digging in the neighbor's yard with a backhoe, scooping out soil and sifting down dirt like coffee grounds. Hammer blows sowed the air with a keen pinging. The builders knocked nails into the planks to frame the walls and then raised the frame. A hardhat squatted and bolted the bottom board to the foundation sill. When the construction crew took a break, they sipped from their thermoses. They smoked, passing around the pack, or wedged a plug of tobacco from a puck-sized canister. Jimi Hendrix's "Voodoo Chile" wah-wahed from a boombox, and a carpenter played his hammer like a guitar.

Each morning, while the builders worked, Matt scribbled notes in a spiral note-pad (he left the computer switched off). He watched his hand writing the words in black ink with cursive letters. He thought he could write a story about the construction workers that would be very good and different because nobody wrote much about people like them. He did title the story Tow Away No Stopping Anytime, a fine title, he thought, for an awfully good story. He worked to get their ordinary speech right, not the way they talked verbatim, but words that made you say yes they talk that way, they really do. Then he'd drive the old man into town for breakfast at the diner, and while they sipped their coffee, he thought of writing a story about the waitress and the truck driver. They would fall in love with each other, but the truck-driver just sat at the counter while she filled his cup, and then he'd leave a coin on the saucer while the waitress gazed perplexedly at the man driving his big rig out of the lot. That would be a good ending.

Here and there, Matt and the old man talked. When the old man asked about his job, Matt told him he taught the same five classes each semester.

"I want to write more," he said. "But when I sit down, nothing happens."

As he spoke Matt envisioned himself standing at the front of the classroom and seeing his students' bored faces. He talked so much his face went numb: his cheek stopped moving. At night he woke up, repeating his lecture: that the hardest thing of all was to simply tell a story. Matt's old man was talking about how they could keep in touch when Matt went back to San Francisco. He asked Matt for his work number.

"I don't like to talk there," Matt said.

The old man coughed: "why do you say that?"

"We don't have offices. They're more like stalls."

"I thought they treated professors better."

"I'm lucky to have a space at all," Matt said, "mostly they're reserved for professors with tenure."

"I thought you had tenure."

"I'm not on the tenure track. I need to get on the track first. I could keep working for years and never get tenure because I'm not on the track. Somebody else could come in on the tenure track and get tenure after a few years, while I wait around trying to get on the track in the first place."

"It sounds like a raw deal to me."

"Well, not much else I can do."

Then came the last day of the visit. The morning before the flight, Matt boxed up the computer monitor and packed his suitcase. They drove together down the asphalt lane, crossed the old highway route, and took the gravel road that edged the country cemetery. When Matt locked the car, the old man glanced at him, but never said anything. Matt watched him walk across the grass. His mother's gravesite had settled. The marker sat uneven in the ground, a corner was chipped.

"I never bring flowers," the old man said. His voice crumpled like paper. "But I come when I can. I talk. I say, remember me?" His eyes became watery.

For several minutes, Matt stared at the marker. He read the birth date and the date of her passing away. Soon he'd reach the same age then one day he'd be older. He felt something: the moment of truth? No. He missed her. What would she think of him? Her death still angered him. She'd left him, taking his childhood with her. He never stopped missing her. He wanted to tell the old man this but he kept quiet, it was only for him, this feeling, not to be shared yet. Matt swallowed and stared at the trunk of an oak tree. The dried husk of a wasp's nest hung in the branches. They walked back to the car and Matt unlocked it with the fob and then drove the old man to the house. The old man climbed inside his pick-up truck.

"Wait a second. Let me make sure the engine will start." He twisted the key.

Matt heard the engine crank over and he watched his father stomping down in the truck's cab.

"Now I flooded the engine. Just give me a second here." He gripped the steering wheel.

"Maybe we can visit in the summer," Matt said. "Will you still be here?"

The engine started. "I'll come out and see you."

"You think this thing will get you to the airport?"

"I'll drive this thing all the way to California."

And when Matt heard him say these words, he

almost worried that the old man meant what he said.

"All right," Matt said, "I need to hit the road. Are you going to be alright?"

"I will or I won't."

Matt placed the computer box in the rental car's trunk and then hoisted the suitcase inside.

"Hey," the old man said. He paused serenely. "One more thing: continue."

"What?"

"Just—continue."

Matt waited in silence at the lowered gate of a railroad crossing as a train, which looked as if it could go on for a mile, passed in front of him: a grimy diesel engine hauling freight cars mixed with coal cars. Speak to me, will you? Say something. Matt listened hard, as hard as he could, with every part of himself. The ideas hovered on the perimeter of his mind. He saw his fingers writing. The beginning came and then he was in the middle. Then, heaving and jerking, clanking like plates in a dishwasher, the last box car went lumbering by and Matt watched the rising barriers. He looked up at the rearview mirror. He was not in the middle of a story. He was in the middle of this very long road.

Born in Canada, Sean A. Labbé grew up in the US, in the midwest: Michigan, Wisconsin, and Illinois. He spent two years in Germany, where he served in the US Army and traveled extensively. After graduating from UC Berkeley, where he studied English literature, he taught English in Istanbul, Turkey, before returning to do graduate work in British and American literature at Northern Illinois University and then at Loyola University Chicago, where he received his doctorate. He lives near Chicago, and he and his wife have a son and a daughter. Labbé is currently working on *Frisco II: Icons*, which he plans to finish in the coming year.

Made in the USA
Las Vegas, NV
30 January 2022